FIRE

UNDERGROUND ENCOUNTERS 2

LISA CARLISLE

Find out more about the author and upcoming books online at lisacarlislebooks.com, facebook.com/lisacarlisleauthor, or @lisacbooks.

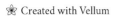 Created with Vellum

FIRE

A Novel in the Underground Encounters series.

I haven't been back since the fire...

Maya Winters, a firefighter, heads out on Halloween to return to her favorite club. A man with haunting eyes watches her, and he's just her type—a dark, brooding bad boy. She feels their connection, but thinks it's merely physical attraction.

Tristan Stone avoids people due to his curse. But when he spots a woman dancing alone surrounded by an unusual glow, he must discover who she is and what gives her the radiating power.

While they attempt to understand their connection, passion ignites. But, the heat could send their world up in flames.

Fire is the second installment in the Underground Encounters series, set in a club that attracts supernatural creatures. Step into Vamps, a thrilling new world of steamy paranormal romance featuring sexy shifters, thirsty vampires, wicked witches, and gorgeous gargoyles.

- *Dark Stranger*
- *Dark Pursuit*

Underground Encounters series

Gargoyle shifters, wolf shifters, and tree witches have divided the Isle of Stone after a great battle 25 years ago. One risk changes it all…

- *Knights of Stone: Mason*
- *Knights of Stone: Lachlan*
- *Knights of Stone: Bryce*
- *Seth: a wolf shifter romance in the series*
- *Knights of Stone: Calum*
- *Knights of Stone: Gavin (coming soon)*

Stone Sentries

Meet your perfect match the night of the super moon — or your perfect match for the night. A cop teams up with a gargoyle shifter when demons attack Boston.

- *Tempted by the Gargoyle*
- *Enticed by the Gargoyle (coming soon)*
- *Captivated by the Gargoyle (coming soon)*

Night Eagle Operations

A paranormal romantic suspense novel

- *When Darkness Whispers*

OTHER BOOKS BY LISA CARLISLE

Underground Encounters series

Steamy paranormal romances set in a underground goth club that attracts vampires, witches, shifters, and gargoyles.

- *Smolder*
- *Fire*
- *Ignite*
- *Burn*
- *More coming soon*

Chateau Seductions

An art colony on a remote New England island lure creative types—and supernatural characters. Steamy para normal romances.

- *Darkness Rising*
- *Dark Velvet*
- *Dark Muse*

Blood Courtesans

A vampire Blood Courtesans multiple author shared World Series.

- *Pursued: Mia*

Visit LisaCarlisleBooks.com to learn more!

Don't miss any new releases, giveaways, specials, or freebies! Join the VIP list and download a free read today!

www.lisacarlislebooks.com

CHAPTER 1

M *aya*
      I hadn't been back since the fire.

Whoever had bought the club had kept the black brick exterior with the painted black windows, ensconcing the club in mystery. Passersby down this hidden alley might think it an abandoned warehouse, unless they got close enough to look up into the recessed doorway to see it flanked by two watchful gargoyle statues.

A moment of hesitation filled me. When I would come with my best friend Nike, I'd never felt threatened. We'd come after long shifts at the firehouse to unwind and dance off some steam. I'd practically bounce down the alleyway so I could get inside sooner.

But now, on my own, the creepiness of the alleyway set in. I wrapped my long black leather trench coat tightly around my body to shield my fishnet-covered legs as if protecting myself. It could be dangerous walking alone through warehouse alleys near the waterfront. No wonder Vamps was hidden back here. You wouldn't want an underground club on the main drag, would you?

My Mary Jane heels clicked loudly on the cement. The further I walked, the closer the clicks were.

Easy, Maya, I chastised myself. *You're going to break into a trot in a second.*

Finally, I made it to the front entrance and pulled on the heavy wooden doors with steel bars intersecting in the middle and was rewarded by a familiar figure.

"Byron, you're still here!" I said to the extra-large bouncer who had an extra-large heart.

"Maya, where have ya been?" He threw his enormous arms wide and I rushed in, aware that I was grabbing him tighter than warranted, probably due to relief after my misgivings walking here alone.

"Whoa, girl, you must have really missed me," he said before he let me go.

"Of course I did. It's been forever. How have you been?"

"Survivin'. Taking odd jobs here and there while they rebuilt this place. You saw the damage from the explosion."

"Yes, I remember." It wasn't something I could forget any time soon.

"Why you here alone tonight?" he asked. "Where's your partner in crime?"

"Nike? I haven't seen her since the fire."

"Are you kidding me? It's been what—a year?" After I nodded, he asked, "What happened with her then? One of the bartenders told me how she saw her go upstairs with the former owner that night. What do you think—they hooked up?"

I didn't know how much to tell about Nike and Michel, even though I was still hurt that I hadn't seen her. Sure, she sent brief emails from time to time, letting me know which country they were in, but it wasn't the same. We were like this—if you could see me, you'd know I was wrapping my index and middle fingers together. Byron was concerned about her, but I also didn't want to perpetuate any rumors.

"Word spreads quickly around here, doesn't it?" I chose to avoid the juicy part of the question and answered, "Last I heard she was traveling around Europe." I left out the part that she was with Michel.

We were interrupted by a couple who opened the door. He was wearing a red velvet smoking jacket a la Gomez Addams, but didn't pull off the look completely with his dirty-blond hair. While they showed their IDs to Byron and paid the cover charge, I glanced at her outfit to see if she was sporting a Morticia-like dress. To my surprise, she was wearing a cowgirl outfit—hat, tassels, boots, and a short shirt. Not a usual costume for a goth club, but she pulled it off.

Note to self: see if you can pull off a sexy cowgirl outfit.

After they passed through the next set of doors, Byron asked, "So you're solo tonight?"

"Hopefully not all night," I lifted an eyebrow. "How's the eye candy in there?"

"You know, the usual. Lots of weirdos."

"Just my type."

"Who you kiddin'? I've never seen you leave with anyone besides your girl Nike."

"Byron. I haven't been out in months. I went on some crappy dates this past year and realized I'm happier just being on my own. All I've done lately is work. Which means the only males I've encountered are coworkers and they smell pretty rank after a twenty-four-hour shift. Since Halloween is on a Saturday this year, and Halloween was always the best night of the year here, I decided to climb out of my self-imposed isolation and make an appearance."

"Well then, get in there and be a naughty girl." Byron smacked me playfully on the ass to push me on. Then he said,

"Wait." He took my hands and extended them out to the side. "Let me get a good look at you. See what outfit you're sporting tonight. Are you wearing a costume under there?"

I cocked my head as I took my hands back to open my leather trench coat shawl, which could fit in just perfectly at a gothic club or a Renaissance fair, but not too many other places. Tonight I was wearing a sexy little pirate wench costume, with a laced-up corset top and short leather miniskirt. "Does this warrant your approval?"

He put his hand on his chin as he sized me up. "Not bad. I've seen you in worse. Still trying to forget the blue velvet gown, black combat boots debacle."

"That was hot," I protested.

He raised an eyebrow before his gaze moved up to my hair. "And you've gone back to black hair, I see?"

"Technically blue-black. There's only so much color I can get away with at work, being a professional and all." I winked. Lately, I'd been alternating between blue-black and a magenta tint, which was about as much as I could manage without the fire chief giving me the look. If I was feeling spunky and wanted to sport a hot pink or blue, I'd wear a wig.

"All right, you get my seal of approval. And you know that's not so easy, princess. Go on in."

I kissed him on the cheek and walked down the dark tunnel lit by candelabras attached to the stone walls. A new sign adorned the door leading to the main club area. Dante's quote was carved into the wood: *Abandon Hope All Ye Who Enter Here.*

"But Maya," he called after me. "Leave some of the pretty boys for me."

"Obviously," I said, with an exaggerated eye roll. "Not my style."

∾

Much of Vamps looked the same, yet much of it had changed. Gargoyles still guarded from their perches around the club. The three smaller dance platforms were replaced by one larger stage. They now had live bands perform up there as indicated by posters adorning the walls. Or when the stage was free as it was now, it was covered with uninhibited dancers who wanted to be watched.

I worried the vibe of the club wouldn't survive the transition. Some clubs try too hard and end up seeming phony. Vamps always had its own style. Some called it goth for the prevalence of goth-inspired dress and music. But they played other music as well. Others called it a fetish club for the revealing leather or vinyl outfits many chose to wear. Black duct tape pasted over nipples has been seen more than once. And the sexy futuristic outfits with hulking boots were a common choice. But to me a fetish club alluded to sex out in the open, which wasn't the case here. I'd never caught anyone doing it—but I have seen some couples get pretty close on the dance floor or in a corner.

I'd call it more of an underground club. One that was frequented by people who didn't stick to conventional dress and music and followed their own path, rather than worrying what other people thought. Whatever the club was, it was where I fit in.

Continuing to look around and assess the club, I thought it still had an authentic feel. The red marble bar hadn't survived the fire, I noted. But it was still manned—or womanned—by the hot bartender with pink hair and a nice rack. I looked over the drink menu posted above the draft beer.

"What's in a Tempting Fate?" I asked her.

"Southern Comfort, Amaretto, vodka, pomegranate juice,

pineapple juice, grenadine," she rolled out in a velvety voice that was as sexy as she was.

"Sold," I said, banging an imaginary gavel.

"You won't regret it," she said.

After she gave me my drink, I toasted nobody in particular, well, I guess myself. *Here's to tempting fate.* I watched the crowd as I tasted the drink. It was exquisite and I took another large sip. Maybe I'd pay for it tomorrow, but it was *gooood.*

When I heard a remix of Type O Negative's *Cinnamon Girl,* I left my drink at the bar to slink my way amid the gyrating bodies. My favorite band, one of my favorite songs. Tragic that the super-hot singer died so young.

In a sea of black-clad bodies, I blended right in. It had been months since I danced, but I quickly found my rhythm and lost myself in the music, dancing with the crowd. I didn't feel the least bit self-conscious that I was alone.

That is—until I felt his eyes on me.

You know the feeling when someone is watching you and you're suddenly aware of it? That tingling sensation made me look up. A tall guy dressed all in black—naturally—stood alone at the right side of the bar.

Something about that gaze arrested me and I stopped dancing. Dark eyes, almost black, on a face that looked as captivating as Jim Morrison in the Young Lion photo shoot. The black hair was a devil-may-care length, past his chin but not quite to his shoulders. Instead of the rock star's signature black leather pants, this guy was wearing a cape over dark clothing.

His gaze penetrated me. So intense. The eyes of someone who was troubled—maybe haunted.

Why was he staring at me like that? Didn't he know my weakness was a dark, brooding bad boy?

My lips parted as if they wanted to say something. But what did I want to say? And he couldn't hear me anyway.

And then with a swoop of his cape, he was gone.

I stood there for a few more moments trying to process what just happened. Some hot guy in the corner watched me, who then took off with a flourish of his cape?

It seemed very Bela Lugosi-ish—another dark, brooding bad boy. I tried to shake off my confusion as *Cinnamon Girl* ended.

The DJ mixed in a version of David Bowie and Trent Reznor's *I'm Afraid of Americans.* It took me another moment or two to brush off the effect that dark stranger had on me. I thought *to hell with that guy* and then got back into my groove.

Tristan

Although I usually worked in the lab while the club was open, an industrial remix of *Strange Days* by the Doors snapped me out of my project. I couldn't hide out down here all night; time to make sure business was running smoothly upstairs.

Bracing myself for the onslaught on my psyche, I took a deep breath before I walked into the main club area. I glanced around the perimeter of the club, scanning the bar area and the dance floor.

The usual darkness surrounded people, the sadness, the isolation, which I could see so vividly while others couldn't. Their souls crying out to me, draining me. I tried to ignore their pull as I glanced around. The bartenders looked busy. The bouncers looked alert for any drunken jerks acting out of control. The gargoyle statues stood intact, watching over the club from their perches. Their stone eyes could see more than they let on. I'd never seen these guards in their human form, yet heard they'd shift at the sign of danger.

Nothing seemed amiss. Good, I could make my rounds and get out of there and back to the lab.

But then one figure on the dance floor caught my eye. She glowed with a light around her unlike any I'd encountered before. Her bright spirit overwhelmed the darkness that surrounded the others. I watched as she danced, oblivious to those around her. Her light mesmerized me. For the first time I'd been around people other than my family, I wasn't overwhelmed by darkness.

I couldn't take my eyes off her. What was it she had?

Then she stopped and looked at me. Even though the club was dark, her light revealed her eyes were a brilliant blue.

When our eyes met, I saw her more clearly. A sadness buried deep within this bright spirit. Whereas others' pain usually repelled me, her pain filled me with compassion. What was hiding there so deeply within this light? What hurt her? Suddenly I wanted to protect her from any pain.

Her light was magnetic; it drew me in. Now that her captivating eyes were staring back at me as well, I became unnerved.

I turned away and disappeared down the back stairwell. Safely in my lab, I sat in my leather chair in the corner I dubbed the library and thought.

What was she?

What would explain the light?

I scanned the books in the library, on the bookshelves built into a rounded wall modeled after one I admired in nearby Hammond Castle. I had books and books on the supernatural, so I flipped through them trying to find more information on why I saw what I did and what that meant.

I flipped through one book after another, reading by the light from the candelabra, which I found more soothing than artificial light.

What would explain what I just saw upstairs with that

woman? Finding nothing, I closed the book and stared into the flames. Then I closed my eyes.

A vision of her dancing quickly shaped itself in my mind's eye. Getting past the initial shock of her light, I remembered the way she moved, the way she danced unabashed to *Cinnamon Girl*. I saw her hips sway, her arms unfurl into the air as if conjuring up the elements, her black hair wave out behind her as she tossed her head back. I visualized her long legs extend up from those chunky black heels, up, up to the tiniest of skirts in her pirate wench costume. Who wouldn't want a peek?

My curiosity about her was now piqued by my arousal. I felt consumed with a need to see her again. What was she like? I had to get up there and meet her.

I blew out the candles and went upstairs, returning to the dance floor area where I'd last seen her. She wasn't there any longer. I walked the perimeter of the dance floor, looking for her.

Where was she? She should be easy to see with that light. That glow.

Was it gone? Was it just my mind playing tricks on me?

Yes, that would explain it. I'd never seen anything like that before. It couldn't be real. It shouldn't be.

Nevertheless, I scanned the people at the bar looking for my little pirate wench. But she was nowhere to be seen.

I exhaled with a deep sigh of regret. I blew it.

Maya

An hour or two later, I decided my dancing legs were broken back in and were now ready for a rest. I went to the ladies' room to make sure I didn't acquire raccoon eyes working up a sweat out there, retrieved my leather trench coat from coat check, and then pulled a heavy door to walk back up the alley.

Byron was talking to someone dressed all in black. The man's back was toward me and I quickly noted the slightly long black hair on a tall frame like Peter Steele of Type O Negative, at least 6' 3".

Yes, this was a good night to come back.

Although he was wearing a dark cape, I noted his broad shoulders. Capes were donned by many Halloween revelers tonight, much like my recent encounter with that dark-eyed mystery man. Who just happened to be tall, dark, and caped.

Byron caught my eye. "You're not leaving already, are you? It's far too early to call it a night."

"I think I've had enough, Byron. Looks as if I need to break in slowly."

"Mr. Stone, this is Maya. She used to be a regular at the old club. It's her first time back since you reopened it."

When this Mr. Stone turned to me, my insides flipped as if acrobats set up a circus routine. Holy shit, it was the guy who stared at me on the dance floor. The one who gave me weird heart palpitations.

Our gazes caught. His dark, penetrating stare did something to me. Something weird. I was aware of this thing beating frantically inside my chest. How difficult it was to swallow.

Why couldn't I break our stare? That connection was too intense.

"A pleasure," he said. I wasn't expecting such a deep voice, as sexy as Alan Rickman's but with the accent of someone who grew up on the North Shore. Amazing how a sexy accent can affect your reaction to the opposite sex.

He bowed slightly to take my hand and kiss it. The tingle that shot from his hand on mine, his lips on my skin, did something to me that I still can't logically explain.

It really must have been too long since I'd been out and interacting with the male species.

"Mr. Stone is the new owner," Byron explained. "He put a lot of attention into rebuilding the club."

"And you're leaving so soon?" he said, never breaking our gaze. "What a shame. I hope it's not that the club doesn't live up to your expectations."

Several seconds passed while my eyes traveled from his dark ones down to stare at lips that I could kiss for days —"interface with," as the guys at work said when geeking out talking about girls. Suddenly aware that I still hadn't uttered a word, I said, "No, it's not that, Mr. Stone. It looks great. I don't want to overdo it. Haven't used these dancing legs in a long time."

"Please call me Tristan. Come, Maya, I'm not convinced. Let me show you around. Maybe get a drink. I'd love to get input from a former regular to see if we're missing any of the old charm."

He took my hand and warmth once again spread from where he touched me all through my body. I controlled my racing pulse for a moment to turn back and look at Byron. His mouth was half-open in shock, but then he recovered in time to wag his finger in front of his face with a naughty grin.

I shrugged back at Byron before Tristan reopened one of the doors into the main club area leading us back into Dante's Inferno as hinted at by the sign. Tristan led me into the loud music and pulsing energy in the club. What was I getting into?

He pointed out some of the new features of the club, the new live stage and a newer bar. Polished black marble graced the top of a dark mahogany carved-wood bar, with scenes of ancient rites of what looked like naked witches dancing around a cauldron carved into the front panels.

We walked over to the bar and he asked, "What would you like to drink?"

"I tried a Tempting Fate earlier and it was smashing." I tilted my head and peered up at him. "Anything else on the menu you'd recommend?"

He stepped back and looked at me. No, appraised me up and down in an unabashed manner. If another guy looked at me that way, I'd rip him a new one, but when Tristan did it, it made me blush. Set me on fire.

I didn't blush often and I wondered why I did now. Luckily it was dark in here.

"I think you deserve a drink as delectable as you look. But that might be hard to concoct. How about a Hotter Than Hell Bloody Mary?"

"Aren't you a flatterer," I said, aware that I was fluttering my lashes like some flirt. "Do you use that line on all the females here?"

"Never before. Boy Scout honor."

I tilted my head. "Were you a Boy Scout?"

"No. Does that matter?"

I shrugged and took a sip of my drink. "Excellent choice," I said. I looked around the club. "I like what you've done with the place. The little touches make it unique. And the new drinks are extraordinary."

"Thank you."

"No, thank you for buying the club. Saving the place." Seeing all the people on the dance floor, I added, "You've made a lot of people happy."

"I hope you're one of them." He looked at me so intensely that I felt self-conscious.

"I am. This is my favorite place for a night out."

"I'm glad to hear that," he said. "The live music is what I think will really give this place a new life. We had an old punk band in here last week. Wicked fun. You'll have to come and judge for yourself one night."

"I will," I said. As if I needed another reason to come back.

First, this was my number one choice for a night out. Second, the new owner's penetrating eyes and his special attention on me right now reminded me of forgotten body parts that had been out of commission for far too long. And third, I loved live music.

Digital music was one thing. It was convenient and you could listen to just about anything you wanted. Records were cooler. That crackly sound and delicate vinyl gave it a sense of something special in a way. But live music—when you could hear the music surrounding you from all angles so that you could practically taste it. When you could see the sweat glistening on the guitar player's forehead and feel his passion for his song. When you caught the energy of the crowd and jumped or danced with them like some kind of collective orgy experience, well, nothing could replace that.

"Wicked?" I asked. "You must be local. We didn't use that expression where I grew up and I only heard it when I moved here."

"I'm from Salem, originally. But now I live near the club."

"Salem, Mass, right? Not New Hampshire," I said. "We're kind of between them both."

"Yes, Massachusetts. Good ol' Witch City," he said. "Where are you from?"

"San Francisco. I'm a California girl, can't you tell?" I said with a grin. With my Bettie Page-styled black hair and straight bangs, pale skin, and goth makeup, I was as opposite of a stereotypical California girl as could be.

"You're what I hope they all look like."

I looked down again. Why did he keep making me blush? This was not something I did often.

"What made you decide to buy this club?" I asked, changing the subject.

"Every area needs someplace for the people who don't

quite fit in with the traditional boring people who all act the same."

"Would you say you don't fit in with the norm?"

He gave me an impish smile and raised one brow. "God, no." Then he said, "Look what happened to that club in Cambridge. Gone. Replaced by condos. I didn't want to see that happen to this place—have it disappear and be replaced by yet another condo or warehouse."

I looked around the club to imagine it divided into condos that all looked the same.

"That would have been tragic," I said. "On behalf of all the misfits here, I thank you."

He smiled at me in a way that shot pulses of energy through my body. I took a sip of my drink to break the gaze.

"I better get going," I said, standing up. "Thank you for the tour. And for reopening Vamps. I love what you've done with it."

"Let me walk you out," he said. He stood and took my hand in his and led me to the front entrance.

The feel of my hand encased in his warm one did nothing to stop my racing heartbeat.

"Did you drive? Or should I call you a taxi?" he asked.

"A taxi would be great."

While he placed a quick call, I said goodbye to Byron. He gave me a knowing smile, which I ignored. Tristan took my hand again and led me outside.

"It was such a pleasure meeting you, Maya."

"Same here," I said, feeling pangs of regret for saying I had to leave.

The regret was amplified when the stupid taxi arrived and Tristan kissed my hand.

"I hope to see you again very soon."

When I closed my eyes that night, I saw Tristan's dark

eyes staring back at me. The moment when my eyes first met his burned on my memory, as if imprinted there permanently. I wouldn't forget that moment, that feeling, for as long as I'd exist.

Snap out of it, sunshine. You sound like you're in a romance novel.

Then I thought, *What's the harm? I'm awake. I can't sleep. What's wrong with a little harmless fantasy? When was the last time I met someone who inspired such longing? Or straight-out lust?*

I tucked myself in cozy under my pale blue comforter and closed my eyes.

Tristan and I were at Vamps. We were dancing to an upbeat song. *Hard Rock Sofa* by Quasar. Our eyes were locked on each other's, oblivious to the dancing bodies around us.

As the tempo quickened, the crowd's energy rose around us, becoming more and intense, almost frenzied. Our bodies moved closer. Still we didn't touch.

My body was so hot, on fire. Was it from dancing, the energy of the crowd? Or the rising intensity of how badly I wanted Tristan?

We moved closer still. Faces mere inches apart. Eyes still locked. Bodies almost touching.

Almost.

The tempo grew faster. To a feverish intensity.

Closer still. I broke eye contact to look at his lips. Licked my own.

God, I wanted to touch him. Kiss those lips.

The beat was at a peak now. Almost orgasmic.

I looked back into his eyes and saw pure, unmistakable lust.

Touch me, my body screamed silently. Touch me now.

The crescendo broke. And with it, the crowd lost all control, their sweaty bodies flailing about to dance freely.

We followed them. And our bodies moved apart to dance. A wanton, seductive dance.

When the song ended, the DJ spun in a slower one.

Our eyes met again. Our bodies moved closer again. One hand reached toward me. I closed my eyes. Then I felt his hand on the small of my back. Pulling me close. Closer.

A song began playing over this one. It sounded so familiar. What was it?

Oh yeah, it's Black No. 1, a great Type O Negative song.

I should have recognized it right away—it was my cell phone ringtone.

Fuck, it was my cell phone ringing.

Who the hell would call at this ungodly hour?

"Hel-*lo*," I said, making sure the annoyance was apparent in my tone.

Double fuck. It was one of the guys at the firehouse.

"We're short-staffed tonight. Figures, on Halloween. Can you come in for a few hours?"

"It's after midnight. Not Halloween anymore."

"Yeah, but I knew you'd still be up."

I could use the overtime. Pushing my fantasy aside, I sighed before hopping into a shower of the coldest water I could stand.

One thing was clear. I had to see Tristan Stone again.

CHAPTER 2

T*ristan*

Days had passed. I asked myself the same question repeatedly: Why did I let her go?

I ruminated in my lab, running my hands over a marble globe on an end table. I spun it, letting the cool feel of the marble glide under my fingers and closed my eyes. Then I stopped it.

My fingers were in the middle of the Atlantic. Might as well have been in the middle of nowhere.

I should have at least asked for her number or a way to contact her again. Instead, I kept an eye out for her at the club each night it was open, but she wasn't there. Why should I entertain false hope that she'd return? I hadn't seen her there before Halloween night. And there she appeared to me in that light—a vixen dressed like a pirate.

What did she look like in everyday clothes? And would she ever return?

Swallowing some pride, I went upstairs.

"Byron, has your friend returned lately? Maya, is it?" I said.

Byron gave me a knowing smile, which he quickly recovered from. "No, only that one time since the club reopened."

"What can you tell me about her?"

Byron ran his finger over his chin. "I don't know her that well. We would talk when she'd come in with her friend Nike some nights. They both helped get people out the night of the fire. I think they work in some sort of emergency services field or something because they seemed to know what they were doing. And that was the last time I saw either one of them until Maya came back."

"Interesting," I said.

"Why do you ask?"

"I want to talk to her."

Byron smiled that smile again, this time not trying to hide the twinkle in his gaze. "If I see her, I'll be sure to tell her."

Maya

I thought about Tristan all week. Not even the banter with the guys at the firehouse kept him too far from my mind. Luckily, it was a busy week. I had to teach fire prevention and safety to an elementary school and we had a visit from a Cub Scout troop, in addition to the usual calls.

Every night I wanted to go back to Vamps. Would I still feel that excitement that welled up when I was around him? The one that made me hyperaware of my sexuality?

I pictured him walking around the perimeter of the club. I checked the website once to see what was going on. Okay, three times. Any live bands playing? Maybe some band I was dying to see that just happened to be playing there tonight so naturally I would go there to see them. I definitely was *not* there hoping to see the new owner who just happened to be ridiculously attractive.

What about all the women parading around in their tiny, sexy outfits? Usually I loved checking out what everyone was wearing. I never went to Vamps to date so a jealous thought never entered my mind. But now I pouted thinking of all those hot women who would just love to sleep with the new owner.

Damn sluts!

Stop it. What's gotten into you? You sound like some jealous stalker.

Obviously, I needed some distance because even in my head I was already going crazy over this guy. If I stayed away, maybe I'd forget him.

At times like this, I wish Nike was still around instead of gallivanting around Europe doing whatever she was doing with Michel and his perfect ooh-la-la French accent.

I mean, come on. Who else could I talk about this with? I was certainly *not* going to talk about it with the guys at work.

Woe is me, I thought, knowing I was being dramatic. I put the back of my hand against my forehead as I looked at myself in the mirror.

"How sad are you right now?" I said to my reflection.

Settling into my sofa, I grabbed my iPad to compose an e-mail to Nike. Our emails had been brief since she'd left, since I was still hurt about her minimal communication. But I needed someone to talk to and Nike was still my closest friend, even though she was across the ocean or wherever the hell she was these days.

Hey Nike,

How are you doing? I haven't talked to you in so long and it sucks. I miss you big time.

Are you and Michel getting it on all over Europe? On the Eiffel Tower? Leaning off the Tower of Pisa, perhaps? Ha ha.

I can't believe I haven't seen you since last year, on the night of the fire. I went back to Vamps for the first time this Halloween. Byron was there at the front door. He asked about you and says hi.

The new owner rebuilt it well. He kept much of the old charm, but rebuilt the stages differently so they can have live bands now. That's pretty cool, I think. Anyway, thought you'd be interested in our old haunt. And Michel would be interested in his old club.

So, I met the new owner. A guy named Tristan Stone. Tall, dark and ridiculous handsome stranger. Totally my cup of tea. I hate to admit it, but I think I'm smitten. Preposterous after just one conversation, isn't it? Go ahead and slap me back to reality.

But something about him—I don't know how to describe it—but I can't stop thinking about him. I know, it sounds cheesy. But maybe you know what I mean. You turned into jelly when you saw Michel at Vamps that night, not your normal tough-ass self. What is it about us and owners of this club making us forget all reason? Does an irresistible love potion come with the deed?

I don't know if you'll even get this. If you have access to e-mail wherever you are these days. But I just wanted you to know I miss you. And you were the one person I could talk to about things like this.

And to confess how I feel like some psycho stalker because I can't wait to go back and see him again. As if he'd even remember me. Just another visitor to the club. Obviously I need to get a grip.

I hope things are great with you and we'll see each other again soon. Any idea when you're coming home?

Are you coming home?

Maya

I signed out of my e-mail and went to bed. I crawled under my comforter and tried not to think of him.

As I drifted off to sleep, I saw his eyes. Those dark haunted eyes that were imprinted on me. Would I ever forget them?

Tristan

None of my books answered any of the questions about

Maya's light. So, I drove to Salem to have lunch with someone who might—my mother.

We sat down in her dining area with large windows showing off her gardens. Although it was early November in New England and the flowers were gone, Mother ensured she would have the most of her gardens for as much of the year as she could. She called the garden her incomplete canvas, one that she'd redesign throughout the seasons. Brilliant reds of Japanese maples and other perennials now dominated the landscape.

We discussed family matters over light sandwiches that Charlotte brought out. Mother had hired Charlotte in recent months to help her around the house, saying it was too much for her to take care of on her own anymore. Charlotte had lost her husband and looked for a job to keep her mind focused on something besides mourning.

Following the meal, Charlotte brought us tea. Tea was a daily ritual in my parents' house. Mother used it as her salve for all life's matters, her quiet meditation throughout the madness of any day.

"Tristan, something is troubling you. I could sense it since you came in."

I wanted to tell her about Maya, but didn't know where to begin. "Yes, Mother. Something is on my mind. Something I don't understand."

"What is it?" she asked and took a sip of tea.

"It's a woman."

My mother leaned forward, smiling. She'd wanted me to settle down and get married for ages, so any mention of a female had her imagination spiraling. But with my ability, whatever it was, I wasn't a good companion for another person.

"Go on," she encouraged.

"She came into my club the other night. There was something about her that I've never seen before."

"What?"

"She was surrounded by a soft white light. Where all I saw around other people were the usual darkness and shadows, she projected this—glow."

Mother looked me in the eyes for several long moments. I looked down at my tea, which was still untouched.

"Interesting," Mother said. "What happened to the darkness?"

I tried to remember. "I'm not sure exactly. I don't know if it was still there. I was so focused on her that I didn't notice."

"Next time you see her pay attention to what happens."

"I don't know if I'll see her again."

"But Tristan," she said touching my hand, "you must."

"Why?"

"Obviously something special happened between you two. And considering your gift."

"Curse," I corrected.

She ignored my correction.

"It means something. It's something worth pursuing."

"What do you think it is?"

"I don't know," she said. "Drink your tea and I'll read the leaves. Maybe we'll find some insight there."

We drank our tea in silence, caught up in our thoughts. I thought of Maya the whole time. I tipped the cup upside down when I was done so the leaves could slide down the china, leaving a trail as they descended. My mother looked upon these markings as foretelling the future. I'd stopped questioning her method long ago.

"While we wait, let's do a reading," she said.

"Not a full one," I said. "Just one card." She shuffled the cards skillfully as she'd done this hundreds of times. "I wish my gift was similar to yours—how nice must it be to tell people their good fortune."

She looked at me over her Tarot deck. "It's not all hearts and flowers. Most of the time when people come to me, it's because they're troubled. And much of the time, when I read for them, they have reason to be. It's not that easy to see that their worst fears may be imminent and yet try to focus on the positive. Try to help them find a way out of their predicament."

"The difference is that you choose to meet with people. You can help them. I *don't want* this ability. What good is it to see sadness in people? I can't do anything about it! I don't want to see their pain." Why was I raising my voice right now? And bringing up a topic I hated to discuss with her?

"Tristan," she said in a soothing voice. "Some gifts take more time to develop than others. Especially if the person fights it. Maybe someday you'll find what makes your ability so special. Our paths are not always clear at first and you're still so young."

I bit my tongue to stop the retort forming and let her do her thing.

"One day you will do great things. I know this."

"Of course you think that. You're my mother. Nobody else feels that way about me. Especially not me."

She looked at me with a mother's sympathy. Then she said, "Close your eyes. Focus on your concern."

I closed my eyes and thought of Maya and her light. Then I picked a card.

"The Emperor," she said. "Major arcana." She looked up at me. "You want to find some influence over things you have no control over. You're thinking about her; she's thinking about you. You will spend much time together. Working together—maybe having fun together. Ultimately, you must work with her to achieve your desires."

"This is ridiculous," I said, pushing my chair back. "I'm not buying it. I might be wondering about her, but she is most definitely *not* thinking about me. Why would she? And I have been alone for almost thirty years. Someone is not going to walk into my life now and change everything just because of what you see on some card."

She just smiled at me and picked up my tea cup to examine the leaves. She turned the cup around slowly and humphed here and there.

"What is it?"

"I'm not sure," she said and looked up at me. "Can you bring her here?"

"Bring her here? I don't even know how to contact her. Why on earth would I bring her here?

She put down the cup and looked me straight in the eye. "I want to meet her."

Maya

One week went by. Saturday night. I wished I was spending my evening getting ready to go to Vamps and seduce one Mr. Tristan "Smoking-Hot Guy" Stone. But I was a working girl. So instead, I sat around in a firehouse, the only female working with a bunch of guys. Although I was usually one of the first ones to engage in the friendly banter that kept us entertained during the dragging moments, lately I was distracted by other things.

Bob Walker, a middle-aged firefighter, noticed I wasn't my perky old self. After most of the guys went out on a call and it was only the two of us left, he asked, "What's with you lately? Most people can barely get a word in when you're around. You haven't said two sentences in a row all week."

"Things on my mind. You know, things."

"I know what that means," he said with a smirk. "I have

two teenage daughters. I don't need a crystal ball to see that by 'things' you mean a guy."

I frowned. So much for keeping my angst to myself.

"Do you want to tell me about it?" he asked.

As a matter of fact, I would have liked to spew out all the racing thoughts in my brain to someone who would just listen to me ramble. But then that would require spilling the beans on the part of my life where I liked to dress in sexy outfits and go to underground clubs. And that would not go down well in a firehouse full of guys, for me at least. Endless ribbing and inappropriate questions would ensue.

"Thanks, but there's nothing to tell."

A couple of emergency calls distracted me during my shift. An old woman who was having trouble breathing had to be taken by ambulance to the hospital. Also, a teenager who was freaking out on drugs had to go in.

Another week went by. I had two days off in a row midweek. I checked the club's website once, okay every day, to see what was going on, but then reminded myself to snap out of it. Instead I spent one night having dinner catching up with a friend and the other one going to the movies on my own.

Saturday night finally came again. Whenever Nike and I had Saturday nights off, we'd go to Vamps as it was the best night of the week. I wished she was with me now for some moral support at least, but there was someone else I wanted to see that night even more.

I paid particular attention to my appearance that evening. After a long, hot shower where I groomed myself as meticulously as if I had a lover awaiting me that evening, I then spent another forty-five minutes trying on outfits. One by one they went from my closet to my body, and then after being rejected, tossed onto an armchair.

"Ugh, stop acting as if you're in middle school and just pick something," I admonished myself.

Finally, I decided on a form-fitting black dress, with Asian red floral satin accents down the front and back where the dress laced together and a slit that reached halfway up my thigh. Sure the black would blend in with everyone else, but the red gave it a little punch. And I wanted to be seen by someone in particular. Not stand out in a bright red, look-at-me, va-va-va-voom number, but one that gave me a little differentiation from the crowd.

I straightened my still-black hair until it went halfway down my back and then gave it a little curl at the ends with a fat curling iron. I ironed my bangs straight, Bettie Page-style. Then I was extra careful making my face up. I lined my blue eyes with black eyeliner to set them off and used plenty of mascara, then softened them with a smoky gray eye shadow. Lipstick tonight called for fire-engine-red. In order to act like a seductress, I had to look like one. And the first person I had to convince was myself.

I looked in the mirror and smiled. For someone who'd been sporting firefighting uniforms or schlepping around in lounge pants and tank tops the rest of the week, I had made quite the transformation from a regular girl next door to vixen.

Damn, I look hot!

I took a cab to Vamps and experienced the familiar urge to bounce down the alley in anticipation for what lay ahead that night. I practically threw open the big door at the entrance.

Byron smiled widely. "Maya, Maya, Maya. You're back."

"Hi, Byron. How's it going?"

"Things have been—interesting," he said. "Someone was asking about you."

My heart beat faster and I tried to control my excitement. After all, it could be some random guy.

I tried for nonchalance. "Oh really, who might that be?"

He cocked his head. "Come on, Maya. Don't play coy."

"I don't know what on earth you mean, Byron." I opened my eyes wide for an innocent effect.

"Save it, sunshine. I'm gay, remember? Womanly wiles don't have any effect on me."

My wide-eyed look immediately was replaced by a pout, without me even realizing what I was doing.

"What's up with you and Mr. Stone anyway? "Byron asked.

Yes, it was him! He asked about me. I mentally jumped in the air clicking my heels like some kind of leprechaun. Then said, "Nothing. Why do you ask?"

"Mr. Stone is one of the most introverted people I've ever met. He stays down in his office or whatever he has downstairs and just sweeps through the club like a bat out of hell to make sure everything's going okay. Don't tell him, but that's what the staff calls him behind his back."

"Bat out of hell?"

"Yes. He scared the crap out of one of the bar help one day, who was replenishing the bottles behind the bar. Mr. Stone came up to check on things and he was wearing his usual black. He flew through the club and then he disappeared downstairs. That's how he usually acts. He does not talk to women and he does not take their hands to give them private tours of the club, like he did with you."

"Uh, um, oh," I stammered. "Maybe he was just being polite because you knew me."

"Maya, please. Why would the owner of a club care who the bouncer is friendly with?"

"Um." Good point. I had nothing.

"Exactly." He nodded as if thinking to himself. "He wants me to tell him when you return. You okay with that?"

Okay with that? I was hoping that he'd at least remember me. The fact that he asked about me and had given me special treatment made me want to spin some Olympic gymnastics flips off the rafters.

"Yeah, sure," I said with a wave of my hand, trying to play it cool. Then I killed that objective with my next line. "Byron, how do I look? Be honest."

Byron looked me over and a grin spread across his face again. "You look smashing. A total fox. If I was straight, I'd be all over you."

"Thanks," I said. "I'm going to get a drink. For some reason, I'm kind of nervous."

"You—nervous? First time for everything, I suppose," he said, shaking his head incredulously. "Go on in. I'll wait a little while before I tell him."

I went to the bar and checked out the drink list again. When I saw a Hotter Than Hell Bloody Mary, I smiled, remembering when Tristan suggested it. But there were so many new mouthwatering choices on the menu. What would I have next? I'm the type of girl who tries everything, not one who orders the same thing every time she goes to a restaurant.

"I'll have an Anything Goes," I told the sexy bartender.

Time to brace myself for anything that could happen.

A few songs later, Tristan hadn't appeared and I had almost finished my drink. Patience wasn't my strong suit, especially when it came to waiting for a guy.

Okay, maybe Byron got caught up at the door and didn't have a chance to tell him yet. Or maybe Tristan was caught up in something and wasn't going to stop everything and jump just because I walked into his club. Or maybe his interest had waned and he wasn't going to come up. The more I waited, the more my impatience grew.

Fuck it. I'm not going to wonder. I refuse to be that kind of girl. The kind who sits around making excuses waiting for some guy to show up. Vamps was my place to let loose and unwind from work, not get caught up in some romantic drama. Look at the toll this pining had taken on my psyche over the past couple of weeks. And for what? Nothing. Nothing but expectation, which did not look as if it was going to be met tonight.

Time to reclaim why I started to come here to begin with. To dance, to be free, to let the real me come out.

I walked out onto the dance floor and found a nook in the crowd that I made my own. It didn't take me long to get into the music. Forcing thoughts of Tristan aside, I lost myself into Billy Idol's *Flesh for Fantasy* mixed into some industrial track of a woman singing about her own fantasies. Then I made up for the last drab year of my life by dancing with wild abandon.

Tristan

When Byron called me to tell me that Maya was here, a part of me froze. I'd been waiting for her to return for days. But now that she was back—what the hell was I going to do?

Now I couldn't really go up to her and ask her probing questions about herself without setting off some red flags. Nor could I tell her about my abilities without her thinking I was some freak before she ran out the club never to turn back.

And I definitely couldn't tell her about that much more illicit thoughts that had crossed my mind since I'd met her.

Screw it. Perhaps that light was just a freak thing, someone might have slipped something into my drink. Maybe I'd go upstairs and she'd appear to me just like everyone else and whatever spell she'd cast on me would be broken.

Only one way to find out for sure.

I steeled myself and walked upstairs. Byron said she was at the bar. I walked up and down the bar, but didn't see her.

Had she already left?

I patrolled the perimeter of the dance floor. The sea of dancers dressed mostly in black were surrounded by that darkness only I could see. The dark auras moved so fast they looked fluid, like liquid shadows flowing around them.

And then I saw the light.

Maya dancing amid the darkness, her white light unmistakable, proving that last time was not a drug-induced vision or a hallucination. The darkness on the dance floor had disappeared, whether it was gone or I just couldn't see it anymore. People looked like people. Had she somehow chased it away?

She moved freely to the music, as if without a care as to what anyone around her thought. She faced away from me, but I knew it was her from the glow. She was wearing a black dress laced up the back with red. Wider openings in the top led to more narrow ones near the bottom as the fastenings cinched down near her waist and over her ass.

Seeing bits of her skin peek through the fastenings teased me. When my gaze travelled over the portion covering her ass, I pictured myself untying the red laces.

The song *Paralyzer* came on and she turned my way. When she danced, she moved as if one with the music. She raised her hands to the air while swaying her hips seductively, yet at the same time, not knowing the effect she had on her audience.

Which consisted of me. Utterly entranced.

Her free spirit was infectious. And her seductive moves were intoxicating. I couldn't take my eyes off her. Her face, those eyes, her curves in that dress, those long, long legs. Unable to resist her draw, I pushed my way through sweaty dancing bodies to get closer to her. Her back was toward me.

I tapped her shoulder and bent down to her ear. "Hello, Maya."

She froze. Then she turned back to look at me. Her midnight blue eyes shined like gems that reflected her light. It was my turn to freeze.

Paralyzed.

Although I'd always thought the song was hot, I also thought it was a little cheesy—falling for someone in a night-club? Come on. But now I felt the song as if it was written for this moment, for me and Maya. Who cared that maybe dozens of other people felt the same way about a partner they desired right now? For me, it was for Maya and me alone.

Recovering from the momentary stillness, I swayed across from her. I rarely danced, but something about the way Maya lost herself in the music convinced me to join her. Her mouth dropped halfway open, but after about two beats, she resumed dancing.

While we danced, our eyes remained locked. I became lost just gazing into those brilliant eyes. Spellbound. What was it about her that entranced me so?

Her brightness had faded to a pleasant glow, like a soft reading light. I remained fixated upon her, not even wanting or daring to look at anyone around us.

My desire for her overwhelmed rational thought at this point. I reached one hand around her lower back and pulled her closer to me. I admitted, "I've been thinking about you."

Her eyes fluttered and closed briefly in such an erotic gesture that I grew hard.

When she reopened them, she asked, "You have?"

I nodded. "Often." Then I grinned at a private joke. "You must have bewitched me."

"I'm no witch," she said, smiling back so brightly that her eyes twinkled. "Just a working girl who likes to dance."

"You do it so well."

"Thank you. Kudos to the DJ," she said, nodding in his direction.

Our bodies quickly synced as they swayed as one to the music I saw the want as her eyes darkened, a look that was surely reflected in my own. It was simply the most sensual dance of my life.

Maya rose onto tiptoes and moved closer to my ear. "I have a confession. I've been thinking about you too."

Surprised, I said, "Have you now?" When she nodded, I said. "All good things, I hope."

She looked down before looking back up with a mischievous look. "All good. And maybe a little bad. Or naughty."

Good God, did she know the effect those words just had on me?

She wrapped her arms around my neck, entwining them around me like a gorgeous serpentine. Just the feel of her arms around me was enough to make me want to moan.

"A naughty girl. Just what I like. And one who can dance as sexy as you."

"I dance sexy?" she asked, a confused look taking over the naughty glint.

"Almost too much for a man to bear," I said.

While we danced with our eyes still locked, I grew painfully aware of my growing erection just centimeters away from her luscious body. How I wanted to press myself against her, into her. People around us be damned. I wanted to throw her onto the floor and take her then and there.

No. I wanted to take my time with her. Take her down to my lab, explore every inch of her.

Surveying her body was a mistake. Her breasts were pushed up against the lace bodice and at my angle, I could see them at a great advantage. A deep groan escaped my lips. Luckily, it was drowned out by the song.

My eyes moved back up to her face. She was wearing such spiked heels that her face was mere inches away from mine. And her lips. She had painted them a sensual red. Now I couldn't take my eyes off her lips.

Then she licked them. Whether intentional or not, I don't know.

But I didn't stand a chance.

I didn't care who was around. Or that I owned this damn club and had employees here working for me. I pulled her closer, so our bodies pressed against each other.

God, how I wanted to kiss her. I leaned in closer, shortening the space between us until they were less than an inch apart…

CHAPTER 3

M *aya*
Holy crap! He was so close, so enticingly close, I could barely think.

My body ached to touch his as I moved with the music that penetrated my senses from all angles. My brain knew there were dozens of dancing bodies surrounding us, but I couldn't see them, so caught up in my need for Tristan. My earlier fantasy popped into my mind. Funny how my fantasy didn't prepare me for how I could want someone so much that I didn't give a flying fuck who was around me.

Tristan's hands moved down to my lower back, hesitating. I pressed my body against him, egging him on. When I felt his erection against me, I gasped. His need for me was just as clear. He ran his hands down over my ass and pulled me in even closer.

I ran a hand through his dark, tousled hair while trailing the other one down his back. As our hands explored each other's bodies, I thought he might pick me up any second. I'd probably wrap my legs around him, if the dress allowed.

Enraptured by my desire, I'd forgotten we were in a public place—the dance floor of his club.

He pulled back and looked in my eyes. "Damn, I want you, Maya, but—not yet."

I slowly opened my eyes from their half-hooded state and tried to locate the part of my brain that controlled speech.

"What is it?" I asked.

"There are other matters involved."

"Matters?" I raised an eyebrow. "Involved?"

"Come with me," he said and grabbed my hand abruptly, leading me to the exit. Then he stopped, let go of my hand, and turned back. "I mean, will you please come with me?"

One part of me scolded not to go someplace alone with a man I didn't know well. Another part, one that lacked all common sense at the moment and operated only on primal needs, nodded.

He took my hand, more gently this time, and led me out a back door of the club. "It's hard to speak in there over the music. And what I want to talk to you about is not something you want to shout out in a loud club."

We walked away from the warehouses and down toward the waterfront. I wondered where we were headed, but we didn't speak as we walked hand in hand.

Tristan turned to me and grinned like a schoolboy. "I'm glad you came with me."

I couldn't help but smile back, and then turned away, running my finger over my bottom lip. "Sure. Where are we going?"

"Hold on. We're almost there." He led us to an old cemetery enclosed by a black iron fence.

"A graveyard?" I asked with incredulity. "Why on earth are you taking me here?"

He walked over to a back corner where there was an opening in the fence and crawled through.

"I want to see something. And I want to see what you feel," he said. "Wait here a minute."

He walked into the middle of the cemetery and glanced around. What was he looking for? My gaze followed, drifting over dozens of old gray tombstones. Some with cracks, others with pieces broken off. The newer plots had gates surrounding family plots or mausoleums. I glanced at him, but the look on his face was difficult to read. A little sad, a little scared, and maybe a little repulsed. Troubled.

After a few moments, he walked back over to me. He reached his arm out for me to climb in with him.

I hesitated. Why was he taking me into a cemetery at night and what the heck was he talking about? *What I feel? What does that mean?*

"What are you doing?" I asked. But I gave him my hand anyway.

I crawled through the opening, which was no easy feat considering how tight my dress was, and then followed him into the graveyard.

"Shh," he said. "I need to concentrate."

He glanced at me and then around me. He turned a complete 360, and then he looked all around the area surrounding me again.

"Interesting," he said.

"What's interesting?"

He didn't answer me, but under his breath, he muttered, "I wonder."

"You wonder what?" I asked.

He locked his gaze on me with a curious glint in his eyes. "I'm trying to figure out why it happens. What are you?"

"What am I? I'm a woman. A very confused woman right now. What else would I be?"

"No. You're not an ordinary woman. You're different."

"You're not going to give me a line that I'm special or

something, are you?" I said. "Because I think after that dance, we should be well beyond pick-up lines."

"I didn't say special and it's not a pick-up line. I said different."

"Oh yeah. That's right," I said with a wave. "I know. We're different from the general public. We're freaks. We hang out in a nightclub wearing weird outfits because we fit in with the other freaks."

"That's not what I mean, Maya. I know why I'm different. But I don't know why you are."

"You're not making sense."

"Just follow me."

He brought me into the middle of the old cemetery to a concrete bench. Tombstones here dated back to the late sixteen hundreds, many carved with winged skulls. Most were slanted and cracked.

"Close your eyes," he said.

I did.

"What do you feel?"

"Utterly confused."

"No, Maya. Focus. What do you *feel?*"

I took in a few deep breaths and concentrated. "A little nervous. I mean it does feel kind of scary to close your eyes at night in the middle of the cemetery. And a little forbidden. As if we're teenagers running around in the shadows. And to tell you the truth—and maybe this is easier to say because my eyes are closed and I can't see your intense eyes—but I'm also a little turned-on."

"This turns you on?" he asked.

I opened my eyes. "A little bit. I mean, you're hot and we're alone, and it feels naughty." Then I sighed. "There you go again, looking at me with those eyes."

"I'm just looking at you. Listening to you."

"It's the *way* you look at me."

"Does it bother you?"

"No. It disarms me. Makes me forget what I was thinking, like I lose all rational thought. Hold on, I'm thinking of the right word. *Titillated* might be the right word for what I feel right now. Is that weird?"

"Not to me," he said. He leaned closer. "To tell you the truth, I'm just as *titillated* right now. And it has nothing to do with the cemetery. It's because I'm with *you*. And because of that dance. Do you always drive men so wild with need when you dance with them?"

I shook my head. "Definitely not." In all my time going to Vamps and all the guys I'd danced with, I'd never danced with anyone like *that*. And I'd never felt such a connection to someone I'd danced with before. Whether it was just erotic or more, I didn't know.

What kind of spell was Tristan putting on me?

"Thank you for coming here," he said. "I know it seems like an odd request, but it means a lot to me."

"Did I help answer your question?" I asked.

"Some of it. There are many questions still to be answered. But right now, that's not what I'm thinking about."

"What *are* you thinking about?"

"You," he said in a breathless voice. "I take it back. Being here with you right now is just as hot as being on the dance floor, but in a completely different way. Can I show you what I'm thinking of?"

I gulped. Unable to respond, I nodded.

Tristan ran his hand along my thigh and my breathing escalated. He leaned forward and his breath warmed my neck. Excitement shot through my body, drawing awareness between my thighs. I instinctively tilted my head back to invite him in and was rewarded by the feel of his sensuous lips grazing my skin.

Yes. Oh yes.

I closed my eyes to revel in the sensation of his lips on me.

Then he abruptly stopped. "Sorry, Maya, I don't mean to blow hot and cold. I brought you here for a reason. And not to seduce you in a graveyard. Even though that's what I want to do more than anything else right now."

It took me a minute to slow down my breathing and control my frustration.

"Everything is getting so confusing," he said. "The way I feel for you. It's all happening at once."

What was happening? My frustration morphed into excitement when he said how he felt about me. Was it possible I had the same effect on him that he had on me?

"I need to tell you something about me."

Oh no, these conversations never went well. "Damn it," I said, turning away. "I knew this was too good to be for real. You're married."

"No."

"Kids."

"No."

"Oh God. Let me think," I said, standing up to pace. "You're dark and mysterious and all. You're ridiculously good-looking. You're a solitary soul, you hide away from people. You wear a *cape*." I stopped pacing and turned to face him. "Holy fuck—you're a vampire!"

"Good God, Maya. Once again, no," he said, putting his hand on his forehead. "A vampire? For someone so enticing, you can also be pretty damn exasperating."

I opened my mouth to protest, but then shrugged. No sense arguing the truth—well, for the exasperating part at least.

"Will you be quiet for two consecutive seconds so I can tell you?" he asked.

"I'm sorry. It's just—you know."

"No, I don't know. But I know what I'm trying to tell you is difficult. It's something I haven't told anyone outside my family. And you're not making it any easier."

I sat back down wondered why he'd tell me. We'd only just met.

Don't overanalyze, Maya.

"Okay, I'll shut up now. See—zipping my lips." I motioned my fingers across my lips.

"About time, my mouthy little firecracker. Although there are many things I'd like to do with those lips, right now I want you to keep those pouty things under control."

I opened my mouth to protest once again, but remembering my vow of lip zip, closed it again and smiled sweetly instead.

He took in a deep breath and closed his eyes for a second. Then he reopened them and put a hand on my knee. "What I was trying to say earlier is that I'm different, Maya. And I think you are, too."

I raised my hand.

"What are you doing?"

"Raising my hand to see if I can speak."

His mouth dropped open. "You are something else."

I shrugged. "I was just going to agree with you. If you mean different in the lovable misfits kind of way. Because if that's what you mean, I get it."

"That's not what I mean." He turned away and muttered under his breath. "How can I describe it?" He turned back to me and asked, "Do you *sense* anything?"

"What do you mean?" I asked. "Like spirits or things like that? No. I don't. Come on. Why would I? I don't believe in that stuff."

He looked taken aback.

"Because when I first saw you, I saw something with you I've never seen in another person before."

I leaned forward. "Really? Like what?" I said it more sharply than I intended, probably due to a combination of sexual frustration and curiosity, both of which were at an all-time high at the moment.

"A light. When I first saw you on the dance floor, you were surrounded by light."

I raised my eyebrows. "What do you mean? Was a spot-light on me or something?"

He shook his head. "No, not at all. I see things, Maya. Shadows, darkness. Around people. I can see their sadness, their grief."

I blinked my eyes rapidly. "What are you talking about?

"For me, it's not just a feeling. It's something I can see. A visible presence around people. And it's draining."

"You see *feelings*?"

"Kind of. But not really. It's more like a presence."

"Like an aura?"

"Don't I wish." He shook his head. "That might be kind of enlightening. But I don't see colors, only shadows."

"Don't you see good things, too? Like happiness?" I asked.

"No. It's not like that. I wish it was. I think I must have been cursed. I've only seen darkness around other people and felt their sadness. Until I saw you."

Whether that was true or the smoothest line I'd ever heard, I didn't know or care. My insides turned liquid with fiery heat.

"Tristan, I don't even know how to process what you're telling me right now. All this stuff about light and darkness. I don't know if it's real or some really twisted shit to see how gullible I am and how much crap I'll believe."

His expression turned grave. I smiled to myself. Appropriate considering we were in a cemetery.

"This is not something I'd joke about."

His serious tone caught my attention. "Okay, if it's true,

what you're telling me, it isn't a part of my world. And to tell you the truth, I need some time to try to understand it. But not now." I raised both arms and dropped them. "Because for the love of God, if you don't kiss me soon, I might just downright explode into a thousand frustrated little pieces."

His eyes moved from my eyes down to my lips. He ran a finger along my lower lip and I squirmed on the concrete bench, wanting and waiting for more.

And then, thank God, he leaned toward me. And finally, *finally*, his mouth was on mine.

His lips were so soft at first, gently testing, caressing. Then, as he began to explore my lips more, our kiss grew bolder, more intense. I put my arms around his neck and leaned into him, sinking into his arms. All the wondering and pining of the last two weeks came pouring out of me as I responded eagerly and melted into this kiss.

His hand ran down my side and up again, venturing to one of my breasts. As he caressed it, I moaned with pleasure, wanting more.

When his lips left mine, I sighed. Why did he have to stop? But when he placed his lips on my neck, I burned with need. He planted soft kisses along my neck, and then sucked on the flesh there as I writhed under the touch of his lips.

He continued kissing down my neck, down to my chest, while he caressed my breast. When he kissed the top of my breasts, which were pushed up to great advantage in this sexy dress, I let my head fall back.

Oh, so good.

Within moments, I had leaned farther back on the stone bench. Somehow we made it onto the ground. He lay on top of me on the cemetery ground, kissing and fondling my breasts while I tossed my head to one side on the dirt. I didn't care about how much time I spent on my hair and outfit right now. The intended effect had worked. I had the man I wanted making me feel like the sexiest woman alive.

I opened my eyes and caught a glimpse of the moon overhead. Full, bright and so close to the Earth right now.

"Look at the moon," I said. "It's so beautiful tonight."

Tristan looked up. "Bella," he said. "Almost magical. But not as beautiful as you."

He kissed my breasts, lightly nibbling on them through my dress.

"Ohhh," I moaned as he kissed from my breasts to my midriff. "That feels so good."

He placed one hand on my knee. Then he moved his hand up to caress my thigh.

"Your lips, your breasts, your thighs," he said. "I wish I had more hands so I could touch all of you at once."

I relished the idea of his hands, his lips all over me. "Good thing you don't. I might not be able to take it."

"I'd like to give it a try."

I spread my arms out to each side. "Then I'm not stopping you."

Then I closed my eyes to savor the sensation of his hands running over my body, his lips on my skin. When his touch descended on different parts of my body, my skin tingled, no, ignited. Commanding the fire within me.

"You feel so good," he murmured.

Something about being out in the open the way we were heightened my senses. The salty scent of the Atlantic Ocean. The soft, sensual touch on my skin. And the awareness we could get caught at any moment. It was so forbidden, which made it all the more erotic.

My senses were interrupted by the sound of people approaching. "Someone's coming," I said, sitting up.

CHAPTER 4

The reality of people catching us hooking up in a cemetery pushed away the erotic aspects I felt moments before. Their voices carried the loud cadence of people who have had a few too many drinks and had forgotten about volume control.

"Shit," Tristan said. "Come on, let's get out of here."

I tried to readjust my clothing as I stood up.

He took my hand and led me back toward the opening in the fence where we had crawled in. Seconds after we made it out onto the sidewalk, we saw the motley band of revelers pass in front of the cemetery gates. Three men all in black and two scantily clad women. They were probably coming from Vamps.

Yep, they would have easily have seen us had we stayed where we were.

Tristan nodded at them nonchalantly as they passed us.

From sexy to smooth. My kind of guy.

Tristan took my hand and led me toward the ocean. We walked hand in hand, lost in our own thoughts.

I broke the silence. "I love the ocean. I've lived on both the Pacific and Atlantic coast."

"I'm glad you chose this one."

"Me too," I agreed. "I love Cat's Cove."

Caterina's Cove on the coast north of Boston had the charm and feel of many of the towns on the North Shore. The warehouse district where Vamps was situated was surrounded by residential areas filled with seaside cottages and small homes. Families had lived here for decades and it wasn't yet discovered by tourists. While the beaches of Gloucester and the artists' colony on Bearskin Neck in Rockport were filled with throngs of tourists each summer, Cat's Cove remained relatively peaceful.

"How did you end up here?"

"When I was in college, some friends and I went on a road trip across the country on summer break. Once we arrived in Cape Ann, I didn't want to leave. So, I moved here after graduating, found work and a place to live."

"Do you miss California?"

"I miss my family but I usually go back every year. My home is here now," I said. "How about you? How did you end up moving here from Salem?"

"Salem's not that far, not as far as California, for instance." He smiled in a way that shot excitement between my thighs. "I learned about real estate investments from my father. Since I was home-schooled, I often spent time in his office soaking it in. Eventually, I helped him with his investments and then investing in properties myself. When I heard of the opportunity to buy Vamps, I couldn't let it pass."

He seemed so young to manage so much.

"A part of me is glad they interrupted us," Tristan said. "Otherwise, I might have taken you right there."

I glanced at the black waves lapping toward us before I grinned at him. "And I just might have let you." I ran my fingers through my hair to make sure no errant graveyard dirt or autumn leaves had taken up residence. "And that would have been bad why?"

He stopped to plant a kiss on my forehead. "That might be hot one day. But our first time together shouldn't be in the dirt. You're too beautiful for that."

I blushed, but then tried to cover it up by changing the subject. "Should we walk back to the club?" I asked.

Tristan thought before answering. "Actually, I live on the next block. Want to come to my loft?"

I smacked him lightheartedly on the shoulder. "You've been luring me back to your place."

"Not so," he protested. "I was just leading us away from the cemetery. And maybe habit brought me in this direction."

"Uh-huh," I said, raising my eyebrows with skepticism.

"Maya," he said. "I'm not one of those guys who lure women anywhere. In fact, I've never brought a woman to my loft before."

This statement momentarily silenced me, but not for long. "Really? Why not? You're a good-looking guy."

"I don't mean I've never been with a woman. I mean I've never brought a woman back to my loft."

"Oh."

"Well. Do you want to come over?"

My heart starting beating quicker again. "Why me? I mean, why am I the first woman you're inviting over?"

"I don't know."

"Well, if that smooth-ass line doesn't convince me, I don't know what will."

"Ha ha ha. Very funny."

"I'm serious. Why am I the first?"

"Because."

"Because?" I prodded.

"Because, I don't know," he said, exasperated. "You're

different. And I've thought about you since I first met you and I don't know what to do with these feelings. All I know is I want you."

It's not often that I become speechless, but actual words could not form in my brain at that moment. Mouth agape, I reached my hand toward him. All I could muster was, "Lead the way."

As Tristan led us by some secluded warehouses near the waterfront, I considered what he just said. Was there anything more intoxicating than an attractive man telling you how much he wants you? My body was all but aflame thinking about where we were headed and what would most likely ensue. The more I pictured it, the more my entire body tingled.

Something about the protective feel of my hand in his, and his isolation that made me want to reach out and care for him. The way he thought of me as someone special struck a chord deep within me. The anticipation mounting inside me was almost too much. The wait was unendurable.

"Tristan," I said.

When he looked at me and asked, "What?" I leaned up to kiss him. I pushed him against the brick wall of one of the warehouses and pressed myself against him as my tongue explored his mouth.

Momentarily surprised, he recovered and responded in kind. I took his large, roving hands and pinned him against the wall like some sort of sexually aggressive predator, a part of me I didn't know existed until this moment. He groaned in appreciation as I kissed his neck, his ears, his chest.

He relaxed against the wall as I explored his body with my hands and lips, both traveling down his torso. His chest and then his abs, so defined I could feel them through his fitted black T-shirt.

My fingers trailed along the waistline of his pants. Then

this brazen vixen within me who had been in seclusion for far too long undid the top button of his black pants. One finger ventured inside. Tristan moaned again and ran his hands through my hair.

The vixen took over as I slid against his body, kissing his torso as I moved down.

"Oh God, Maya," he said. But then he stopped me. "No. Not here." He pulled me up by the arms and I was facing him again. Then he said, "But damn it, I want you." He cupped his hands on my ass and lifted me off the ground and I wrapped my legs around him. He turned us and pinned me against the brick wall, rough enough that I exhaled audibly on impact.

He kissed me harder than before, more intense. Now it was his turn to explore me with his lips and hands. He squeezed my ass as he explored my neck with a skilled tongue. I moaned in appreciation and imagined what else he could do with it.

He ran his tongue down over the tops of my breasts and I silently thanked the gods for picking this outfit that allowed for some cleavage.

I glanced around quickly to make sure nobody was walking this way. And for people in the buildings who just might happen to look outside, well, too damn bad.

"Tristan, this is so fuckin' hot," I said. "Just take me. Right here, right now. Up here against this building."

"You want it here?" he asked, kissing back up to my neck, my sensitive area behind my ear. Could I even respond at this point? "Now?"

"Uh-huh," I managed.

"How bad?"

"Bad."

"You want me?"

"Oh God, yes."

"Even with my—issues."

49

I tossed my head to one side against the wall. "I don't care about your issues right now. All I know is I want you."

Tristan pulled back and searched my eyes. "What about tomorrow, when you remember what I revealed tonight?"

"I don't understand that just yet," I admitted. "But we all have something we're hiding. Something we think makes us so different that nobody could love us."

"Even you?"

"Even me."

"Oh, beautiful, now I'm even more curious. What could possibly make you unloveable?"

"Let's worry about that tomorrow."

"You sure?"

"Definitely." I nodded.

Then with a swoop, he threw me over his shoulder. I let out a yelp and he smacked me on the ass.

"What are you doing, Tristan?"

"Taking you home with me. And throwing you on my bed. Not some cemetery, not against a building—but in my bed. Where I've wanted to take you since the night we met."

When we stumbled into Tristan's loft, unable to keep our hands off each other, the only thing I noticed was a bay window facing the Atlantic. His lips captured mine and demanded more while his hands claimed the most sensitive parts of me.

Through this dance, he led me through the loft. Somehow I knocked over a plant on an end table.

"I'm so sorry!" I said, breaking free of our embrace to tend to the destruction.

"Leave it," he said and we tramped through the spilled dirt over to his bed. True to his word, Tristan threw me on the bed.

"Ooh!" I said.

"Too rough?"

"No. I liked it." I melted into the soft black comforter. "You're right. This feels much better than the dirt."

He lowered the lights. "No cemetery, no brick buildings, no potential strangers peering in on us. I have you here now, alone, in my loft." He pulled off his shirt. "And I'm not letting you go any time soon."

I admired his chest, trying not to ogle. "Luckily, I'm not on call tonight."

"On call," he repeated, while taking off one of my leather boots and kissing my ankle. "For what? What do you do?"

"I'm a firefighter."

He looked amused. "Really?" Then he planted soft kisses up my calves. "I hope you're not planning on putting out any fires tonight."

I'd heard some version of that line fifty times by now and usually responded with a smart-ass comment. But coming from Tristan during this very heightened moment, I could only shake my head in reply.

My heartbeat raced as his kisses moved up my leg. With his lips on my skin, I couldn't think of anything else but my burning desire, growing more intense as he explored my body.

CHAPTER 5

*T*ristan

Her skin tasted so good beneath my lips. I could make out the faint scent of strawberries as I kissed her legs.

All night my body and mind had been at odds. One part of me wanted to probe her with more questions, understand why she projected such a powerful glow. And when I explained how I was different, the weight lifting off me from the confession was elating. I'd never told another person before outside of my own family, for good reason.

Maya didn't shy and run away. She didn't look at me in horror. In fact, after her initial confusion, she glanced at me again with hunger in her eye. A look no man could ever resist.

And that caused the conflict with the other part of me. My body that raged in heat, wanting her so. Wanting to probe her in so many more illicit ways than her mind.

Her secret—whatever it was—only made me want to know her all the more.

Her long shapely legs went on forever, I could kiss them all night. As I kissed and caressed her thighs, she began to breathe quicker. I continued to stroke her soft flesh as I kissed over the dress, moving up her torso and up to her breasts. I kneaded a firm round breast with my other hand, running my tongue along the tantalizing edge where the dress met her skin.

She purred, "Ohhhh, Tristan."

Hearing her say my name in that sexy voice encouraged me to explore further. I kissed and licked her cleavage while continuing to stroke her thigh. As my fingers crept up, I felt her tense in anticipation.

As I touched the lace edge of a panty line, I felt her heat. I ran my index finger up the edge of one side of her panties and then tiptoed my fingers across the top and down the other edge. She writhed under my touch, and when I stroked over her folds, her panties were already wet. I kissed along her jawline and pulled back to look at her—this exquisite woman in my bed. Her eyes were hooded as she looked back at me.

"Are you sure you want to do this?" I asked.

"Yes. Oh yes," she said.

My gaze fell on those pouty lips, half-opened, and I swooped down to kiss them. They were so full and soft I could kiss them all day, but there were so many other parts of her I wanted to explore. While we kissed, I moved my fingers up under the lace of her panties, up over her sex, and stroked her gently. When she moaned softly, I explored the most delicate parts of her, so tight and inviting.

"Ready for me?" I teased.

She nodded a few times before uttering, "Oh God, yes. Uh-huh."

"Let's get these off then," I said, pulling her panties down while she lifted her hips to help remove them. "Roll over."

When she did, I untied the leather fastenings keeping her dress closed, loosening each one as I moved from her upper back to her waist. The lace that teased me on the dance floor when I saw her earlier that night. Was it only a short time ago? The moments I'd spent with Maya tonight seemed to stop time in its tracks.

As I exposed more of her skin, it revealed black outlines of a tattoo. I kissed down the softness of her back and she sighed in contentment. The more I exposed her skin, the more her tattoo was revealed. Some sort of intricate design, like Aztec art, with flames wrapping through it near her lower back. The tattoo continued all the way down.

Unbelievably sexy.

When I unraveled the fastenings covering her ass, I couldn't help but touch her there, squeeze that enticing flesh. I had to pause to regroup since my erection was threatening to take matters into its own hands.

She helped me pull the dress off and then she rolled over onto her back. There she was, fully naked on my bed. Mine.

As I drank in the sight of her, I didn't know what I wanted to touch more—her breasts, her pussy, any part of her skin. I started up with her beautiful round breasts, the perfect size for my greedy hands. As my fingers explored them, touching and squeezing, I ran my tongue over her pink erect nipple, nibbling it lightly. She moaned and squirmed beneath me, encouraging me to explore further.

While I continued to worship one breast after another, I ran my hands down along her pale soft torso, down her tiny waist, down to her soft folds. She was already so wet and eager, I slipped my finger right in, feeling the warmth around me. She continued to writhe and moan, grabbing at my shoulder blades.

"Now. Please," she pleaded.

Since my cock was practically throbbing to get inside her, I didn't need any more encouragement. I quickly tore off my clothes and fumbled around a drawer to find a condom. As I put it on, she reached down to help me, wrapping her hands around my shaft and moaning appreciation. She stroked me gently at first, but then more eagerly. I met her increasing rhythm until I knew it would lead to a point I didn't want to reach too soon.

"If you keep doing that, you're going to make me come. And I'm only just starting with you," I said.

She let go and spread her legs wider, inviting me in. Finally, I entered her in a sweet slow motion to savor the sensation. Heightened sensations rocketed through me, ones I'd never felt.

She tightened around me, exciting me further. I increased the momentum as I penetrated her. The deeper I pumped, the more I wanted.

She murmured something incoherent and then pulled me closer to her, wrapping those long legs around my waist. She met my thrusts with enthusiasm as our pace intensified even more.

"You are exquisite," I said, burying my face into her silken black hair and inhaling the scent of a vanilla shampoo. "And you smell so good."

I never wanted this moment to end. Touching her body was far too exciting.

"Oh Tristan," she whispered.

"I want you on top of me," I said and flipped us so we reversed positions. "So I can see you like this."

When her muscles tightened over my cock, I almost came. Fighting to regain control, I watched her face as she set a steady, exquisite tempo.

"You are so beautiful," I said as I ran my hand along her pale cheek. "Unforgettable. A dark-haired angel with a luminescent glow."

I ran my hands down her cheek to her rounded breasts. Every part of me was intrigued by her—her body, her essence, her soul. What was she? Why did she feel so good, almost magical?

And once again I wondered what secret she had.

My questions were silenced as her breathing escalated and she increased her tempo. Hell, she was exciting. My pace increased with hers until our bodies reached a feverish pitch.

"Oh my God, Tristan," she exclaimed as she contracted around me and covered me with her fluids. Within moments, her orgasm propelled me into a feverish state of no return. I dug my fingers into her hips, pulling her down and not letting her go.

"Yes, Maya. Yes."

She collapsed on top of me and I held her in my arms. Exhausted, spent, and—content.

Half-awake, I found one arm wrapped around Maya. I moved my hand up to stroke her breasts.

My erection drove me toward her and I pressed myself against her ass.

"Mmm," Maya moaned in her sleep, pressing her ass back toward me.

Then my over-analytical mind woke up and ruined it.

I'd never had a woman sleep in my bed before. Everything happened so quickly last night; we just went with it, but didn't think things through.

But she was so damn tempting. I ran my fingers from her breasts, down her flat belly, and over her sex. She was already wet and ready for me. I stroked her lightly and she opened her legs slightly to let me in.

I kissed her neck. This could be a great way to start the day. And many days after this...

No. What was I thinking? There was no place in my life for a woman. I was not a suitable companion to anyone.

Reluctantly, I pulled away from Maya. If I stayed in bed

57

with her, my cock would take over and squash rational thought. I put on some boxers, which did nothing to hide my erection, and went to make coffee. Maybe after caffeine I could think more clearly.

As I watched the coffee drip into the pot, my mind tormented me with all kinds of questions, mostly coming back to *What the hell do we do now?*

Then I looked back in at Maya sleeping so peacefully in my bed. I wanted to crawl back into bed with her, wrap my arms around her and spend the day with her in my arms.

I wanted her.

But we couldn't be together. It would never work. Not with a freak like me.

What the hell do we do now?

Maya

I woke up slowly the next morning, feeling strangely aroused. Wasn't Tristan with me, touching me? Or was that just a dream?

The smell of coffee brewing settled into the room, which never happens when you live alone unless you plan ahead. It was a great way to wake up.

Note to self: learn how to set automatic timer on coffeemaker.

What wasn't so great was that Tristan wasn't in the bed with me.

I closed my eyes again to relive what was a splendid night that started with all kinds of surprises and craziness and ended with hot sex. How the heck did all that happen in just one night?

The sound of Tristan walking into the bedroom made me open my eyes. He was wearing black boxers that let me see up close what a phenomenal body he had. My mouth dropped. Yummy. Funny how we had sex last night, but I didn't get to appreciate him as a whole since our bodies were so intertwined.

"Hot damn," I said.

"The coffee?" he asked, raising an eyebrow.

"I'd love some," I said. "Thanks. But I was talking about how cut you are. What the hell do you do—work out for five hours a day?"

He laughed. "I barely squeeze an hour in. And try for five days a week. What about you? With your fine body, you must do something to keep yourself looking so good. Let me guess —long legs—running?"

"Ugh, no. This body is the result of bad eating habits and sloth," I said.

"Ha. I don't believe that for a second. In fact, you look even more beautiful now with your hair all tousled and no makeup. Very fuckable."

"I don't believe *that* for a second, but thank you anyway."

Tristan fixed my coffee with plenty of cream and sugar, the way I liked it, and then he made us a couple of omelets stuffed with spinach, tomatoes and feta cheese.

"I only have one chair at my table. So how about breakfast in bed?" he asked.

The solitary chair at the table struck a chord deep inside. He didn't have any friends visit? Was he lonely? An urge to pull him into my arms and take care of him came over me.

"Breakfast in bed sounds scrumptious," I said.

"Much like you," he grinned.

We propped ourselves up with pillows and brought our omelet and coffee to bed. Tristan opened the shades to a splendid view of the Atlantic.

"This is incredible," I said.

"The omelet or the view?"

"Both."

While we ate, my gaze alternated between the magnificent view of the ocean and that of the magnificent man in bed with me.

"Tristan, did you ever come to Vamps before you bought it?"

"Yes."

"I don't remember seeing you. And I'm sure I would've noticed someone as hot as you."

"I never stayed long, considering my, uh, condition. It was too draining."

I tilted my head as I appraised him. "I'm surprised you even came at all then."

"I'm so used to being alone, but sometimes even I need to get out and be among people. And it's easy to blend in there."

Once again, I wanted to cradle him in my arms and pull him against my chest. Instead, I put my hand on his shoulder.

"I can understand that," I said. "You're not alone now. I'm here."

"Are you?" His dark eyes implored. "I'm not too much for you?"

"I should be asking you that question," I said with a coquettish smile. "I'm not too much for you?"

"Too much?" he said, and then he pulled me close, planting a kiss on my lips. "I can barely stay focused on this omelet as I just want to get more of you."

I put my plate on the end table, and then put his down on his end. "I'm suddenly hungry for something else."

Tristan flipped me onto my back and I squealed with laughter. "What are you doing?"

"You know exactly what I'm doing."

Then he kissed me right where I liked it on my neck. As his kisses trailed down over my breasts and over my belly, I sighed in contentment.

"Want me to stop?" he asked.

"God, no."

He teased me, kissing down one hip and along my thigh, from one inner thigh to the other, while I writhed beneath him in anticipation. And then finally, finally, I felt his tongue on me, masterfully taking control of my entire body.

Wow. I almost forgot how good that felt. Even better than I ever remembered. Or maybe he was more skillful than my past lovers.

He alternated bringing me right to the edge, and then slowing down and backing off, until I was ready to scream out, "Now—don't tease anymore!" But words failed me. As if sensing my need, he increased the pressure and became relentless, driving me to a point of no return. The world exploded around me in an intense, world-shattering orgasm.

When I came back to Earth, I muttered, "That. Was. Phenomenal."

"Just the appetizer, beautiful."

He grabbed a condom from the end table and within seconds had it on and was inside me. I caught the pace with his rhythm, wrapping my legs around his waist. He lifted my ass off the bed and I met him with each thrust. His cock rubbed me in just the right spot at this angle. My need for him intensified and I took control of the pace from underneath him. Then I squeezed my legs tighter around him as I reached a peak again.

"Oh God, Maya."

He thrust harder, exploding deep inside me. We crumbled back onto the bed, out of breath.

I wasn't sure how exactly to ask the question on my mind without blurting it out bluntly and killing the afterglow. "Can I ask you something personal?"

He rolled up onto one elbow. "What?"

"You've clearly been with other women before. You're far too skilled not to have practiced."

"Thanks, firecracker. You're pretty damned impressive yourself."

"What I'm wondering—is how you managed to be with other women considering your uh, condition, as you call it."

When he chuckled, I exhaled in relief. So, I didn't offend him.

"Very short-term relationships," he said. "And keeping the lights off."

After we refilled our coffee cups and came back to bed, Tristan asked, "Do you have any plans today?"

I shrugged. "I just planned on doing laundry, errands, the typical things you take care of on your day off."

"Maybe I can encourage you to spend the day with me. There's someone who wants to meet you."

Surprised, I asked, "Who?"

"My mother."

After my mouth dropped to the floor, I asked, "Your mother? Don't you think that's taking things a little fast considering we just spent our first night together?"

"The first of many, I hope." He flashed a smile that would make any woman agree to do anything he asked in an instant. "I told her about your light." He put his hands out to the sides. "And I don't know what to say. She asked to meet you."

"O-kay then," I said. "This whole light thing—she gets what you're talking about? Because I sure don't."

"Will you please come?" he asked. "It would mean a lot to me."

How could I resist that imploring look in his dark eyes? I think I might have done anything to alleviate that pain.

Tristan drove me home.

"Want me to wait while you get ready? What do you need, say twenty minutes?"

I tilted my head to indicate the unlikelihood of that happening. Twenty minutes? "Please."

"Thirty?"

I raised my eyebrows.

"Forty-five? An hour? How long does it take for you to get ready?"

"I'd say an hour. But give me an hour and a half, just in case. I wasn't planning on meeting any parents today. I need to dress accordingly."

"You don't have to worry too much about my parents. They're not exactly—conventional."

I wanted to ask him what he meant, but it could wait. "You'll tell me more on the drive there, right?"

"I will. See you soon."

As I climbed out of his black Mustang, he slapped me playfully on the ass. "I'll miss that."

CHAPTER 6

When I entered my apartment, everything changed. I frantically threw aside one rejected outfit after another. What the heck was I supposed to wear to meet the parents of a guy I hardly knew? A guy whom I just spent the night with?

I paced and bit my nails.

Music. I needed music. What I needed now was some sort of confident I-am-woman-hear-me-roar music. I looked through my record collection, but didn't know what I wanted. I played music on my phone, shuffling through songs to find something to fit the mood. When Gogol Bordello's *Pale Tute* came on, I settled for fun upbeat gypsy punk to get me on the go at least, rather than filled with uncertainty about the day ahead.

I wish these guys were in my extended family. What a fun, happy band. Maybe I'd even join the band as some sort of extra. I could dance around singing backup vocals, maybe bang a tambourine. That couldn't be that hard to play, right? You just hit it with your hands, maybe on your hips. All you need is to match the rhythm of the band and not go off on some random beat of your own. We would have fun singing and dancing like Gypsies! Then partying 'til the wee hours of the morning.

Focus, Maya. Why does your mind wander to ridiculous, completely unrealistic fantasies in times of stress? You're not running off to join a Gypsy punk band. Stop looking for the escape just because you're nervous. You're a firefighter and you love your job. And you're meeting some guy's parents this afternoon. Some guy who you are way too into way too soon. But it's too late to worry about such things. So, get dressed!

Why did I agree to meet them anyway? What kind of family were they if seeing me in a light was something they wanted to explore in more depth?

Did I really want to be dissected under a microscope?

I picked up my phone to call Tristan and tell him I changed my mind.

No, I couldn't do that to him. He'd said it meant a lot to him. I couldn't bear being the cause of any more sadness in those deep, dark eyes.

Forget it, I'd pick my outfit after. I hopped in the shower and thought some more.

Meeting parents already? This was too much, too soon. What was I getting myself into? A relationship? Did I even want one?

This was all going too fast. Progressing from a mega-crush to a hot night to meeting the guy's parents within twenty-four hours was just too crazy. *I can't do it.*

After getting out of the shower, I found a flowing black skirt that was both feminine and conservative—perfect for such an occasion. I found a button-down white short-sleeve blouse that fit the bill and set off the blackness of my hair. *I can't do it.*

I looked in the mirror and tried to trick myself. "I *can* do this."

No, I couldn't. I glanced at the clock. Crap, it was too late to call Tristan and cancel. He'd arrive soon. I'd wait and tell him in person.

I brushed my hair and put on some light makeup.

Ten minutes later, Tristan rang the bell. I walked over to the front door to let him in, bracing myself before I broke the news.

When I opened the door, he smiled so brightly that I forgot what I was going to say.

"Ready, gorgeous?"

All my reservations slipped away. *Take his hand and everything will be just fine.*

"Just about," I answered. "Come on in for a few."

Tristan flipped through my record collection while I fished for a pair of matching earrings in my bedroom. Nothing too large, but something demure would work.

"The Velvet Cocks?" he said from the living room.

"One of my favorite bands," I replied. "They're local and great fun."

Ah, simple diamond studs. That was it. I completed the look and stepped out into the living room. "How do I look?"

He flashed a decadent smile. "Good enough to eat."

"Tristan." I sighed. "I need to look parent presentable."

He laughed. "You look beautiful."

We walked to his car and he opened the door for me like a true gentleman. On the drive to Salem, he flipped through music on his phone.

"What is this song? I heard it in that *Mr. and Mrs. Smith* movie. When Brad Pitt and Angelina Jolie are all over each other when they first meet."

"*Mondo Bongo*."

"*That's* what it's called? They don't even say those words."

He shrugged. "Joe Strummer and the Mescaleros. You know—the singer from The Clash?"

"Oh yeah. No wonder his voice sounds familiar."

I was well-aware that we were both procrastinating the big heavy talk. Where all the questions and mysteries from last night were supposed to be explored. We listened to more songs and I dawdled, asking more trivial questions about them.

After I inhaled, I announced, "Okay, I'm ready to hear more."

Tristan cocked his head. "Music?"

"No. You know what I mean. Last night you wanted to tell me things about you. About how you're different."

Tristan tapped the steering wheel a few times before answering. "It's not just me. My family—we're all different."

I adjusted in my seat. "Different how?"

"We," he began, but then he stopped. "We're not like everybody else."

I wanted to ask what he meant again, but then changed my mind and decided to let him tell me in his own way. Progress for a motormouth like me.

"We've been here for hundreds of years. My family was one of the original settlers in Salem."

"Oh," I said. What was so weird about that?

"Some of the women, my ancestors, were accused of witchcraft."

Now I was paying attention. "What happened to them?"

"They were burned," Tristan said and he gritted his teeth. "Or drowned." On the last word, he clenched his teeth.

"That's terrible." I reached up to put an arm on one of his broad shoulders. "What a tragic family history. So many innocent people died."

He looked me in the eyes and said, "Innocent of what? They were witches."

I didn't know what to say.

"They were innocent of wrongdoing, or any of the fabricated charges against them. But yes, they were witches. I come from a family of witches. It doesn't mean we're evil. Just misunderstood. They didn't deserve to die."

I removed my hand. "Whoa. What are you saying? You're a witch? Or a wizard or something?" Signs outside pointed to Salem, Witch City, USA. "Wait, you mean like those high school kids who parade around wearing pentagrams saying they're Wiccan? Or those people who go on talk shows to say they're vampires because they feel the need to drink blood?"

"Never mind all that nonsense," he said, waving his hand, keeping his eyes fixed on the road. "I'm telling you that we're not like regular people. We can do things. We have ancient magic, a spirituality, running through us."

I cocked my head. "What kind of things can you do?"

He clenched the steering wheel before he replied. "Me? I can't do anything of importance. I've been cursed."

After recovering from his statement, I said, "Surely that's not true? Why would you be cursed?"

"You wouldn't say that if you've experienced what I have —it's haunted me for so long. I long to be free from it."

"Do you think there's a way?"

"That's what I've been trying to find out for years."

We drove in silence for a few minutes. Then I asked, "Are you the only ones who are, you know, like you?"

"What do you mean, Maya? Are there other witches?"

I nodded. Witches seemed an odd word to use, especially for the hot guy next to me.

"Yes, there are others. Not as many as there once were, but we're still around. In fact—"

He stopped and didn't continue so I prodded. "In fact what?"

"Never mind."

Now when people say things like *never mind*, it just makes me all the more curious. Why start a sentence unless you're going to finish it?

"No, please continue," I said in a polite tone, even though I was itching to know the truth and wanted to demand *Tell me now!* "You were going to tell me something."

He hesitated. "I was going to say how I thought you might be like us. Maybe your family or something. Because I can definitely sense something different about you. Why else would I see you in a light?"

I flinched, but tried to play it off as a crick in my neck. What he likely sensed about me was something I didn't reveal to others. It wouldn't be considered normal on any scale. "Sorry, Tristan. I'm a firefighter. Not a witch."

We drove past the touristy witch museums and attractions that lured tourists in year-round, but to epic numbers during Halloween. Since it had just passed, the streets weren't chock-a-block, and the drive along the harbor, dotted with sailboats, was picturesque and peaceful. Tristan turned onto a quiet residential street. I marveled at an old Victorian house, then a Federal style, and a lovely Queen Anne. We drove for a few more minutes until we reached a Tudor house with a historical marker on it. Even though it was a modest New England size, not ostentatiously large, it still emanated class and old-world charm.

He held my hand as he led me up the stone walkway and into the foyer. I looked around to see large oil paintings on the walls and small statues of female goddesses on pedestals. *Statues?* Nobody I knew had statues in their houses.

"Tristan, dear," a woman with a striking gray-white bob said, wrapping him in a warm embrace. She turned to me. "You must be Maya," and she surprised me by hugging me as well.

"Yes. Nice to meet you, Mrs. Stone."

"Please, call me Isabella," she said, and then pulled back to look at me as if trying to understand something.

How much had Tristan told her about me?

Isabella said, "Come, let's sit in the courtyard. It's not often we can take advantage of that in November, but the weather has been mild this year." She led us through a dining room with more paintings and an old and expensive-looking table. She opened French doors into a lush garden filled with gorgeous red foliage on dwarf Japanese maples and brilliant red bushes.

We sat down at a black wrought-iron table set. No sooner than I had pulled my chair in than a middle-aged woman approached. She carried a tray with a teapot and fancy china teacups and some cookies.

"Thank you, Charlotte," Isabella said.

Charlotte smiled. "Anything else, Mrs. Stone?"

"No, thank you. This is lovely."

Charlotte disappeared. I was more of a coffee drinker myself, but this fancy setting reminded me of one of those posh restaurants serving high tea or a scene from *Alice in Wonderland*.

What the heck is high tea anyway?

I added two spoonfuls of sugar and tons of cream to my tea. Just as we had all poured and prepared the tea to our liking, a man approached. He bore such a resemblance to Tristan that I did a double-take.

My surprise was clearly registered on my face as Isabella said, "Tristan takes after his father."

My mouth had dropped open. *Get a hold of yourself. Make a good first impression.*

Tristan's father had the same tall frame with broad shoulders, but his appeared to have softened with age. His face was so similar to Tristan's that I thought I was viewing a version of him in twenty-five years, with some laugh lines and a little gray around the temples.

Me likey the distinguished Stone look.

"I can see the resemblance," I replied.

Whereas Tristan wore his hair longer, his father kept his close-cropped, almost a military cut.

"Maya, this is my father, Eric Stone. Dad, this is Maya." He turned to me. "Wait, Maya, I don't know your last name."

Our eyes locked for a moment. I tried to suppress the blush creeping in my cheeks considering all the ways we explored each other, yet failed to share something as simple and elementary as the initial formalities. As if reading my thoughts, Tristan gave me a knowing smile.

"Winters," I said.

Tristan's father said, "Nice to meet you," and excused himself before he left.

My question about how much Tristan had told his mother was quickly answered.

"Mother, I was telling you about Maya. When I look at her, I see light. All the darkness disappears. I took her to the graveyard to see what would happen, to see what she'd feel."

He caught my eye and I'm pretty sure we were both thinking the same thing about how hot things got in there.

"When she walked in, all the spirits disappeared from my vision and I could only see her light. But she didn't feel anything different. What do you think that means?"

"I don't know, Tristan. Gifts are different for everyone. Maybe she has an affinity with some type of good spirits. Or maybe her gift is a connection with you. The light to your darkness."

She turned to me. "Tell me, dear. Have you ever felt you were different from others?"

"Well yes, but no, not really."

"How about your family? Anyone have any special abilities?"

"No. But that's natural."

"Why do you say that?"

"I was adopted. So, there isn't a biological connection between my relatives and me."

She looked at me sympathetically, which people often did when they found out. I hated that. As if I should be pitied. It wasn't intentional, but still. I love my adoptive parents, and the speculation made me protective of them. They gave me so much love and support that my biological parents probably weren't able to give for one reason or another.

"I see," she said. "Do you know your biological parents?"

"No. I don't know anything about them," I said, lifting my chin up. Sure, I wondered about them and why they'd given me up for adoption, but nobody needed to know that.

She opened her mouth as if she was going to ask a follow-up question, but then changed her mind.

We talked about my life for several minutes longer and this conversation was turning out to be more like one between two women meeting for the first time rather than one trying to figure out if the other had any special gifts. Tristan sat quietly, his eyes focused on me. Isabella then asked, "What do you do for a living?"

"I'm a firefighter," I said.

"Interesting career choice. What drew you to that?"

"I've always been fascinated by fire," I said in a measured tone.

The three of us exchanged glances. They seemed to sense there was something more to it.

She put her mug down. Tristan leaned forward.

"Since when?"

"Since always," I said.

"Please. Will you tell us more?" Isabella said.

I had to think about that one. This was something about me that nobody knew outside of my family. Our little secret. Not even my best friend Nike. It's not something I could share. They would think I'm nuts. But since, Tristan thought

I'd think the same thing about him and run away, I had to give them the benefit of the doubt. If anyone would understand being different, it was this family.

I took a deep breath. "Here goes."

Tristan

Although I knew Maya was special, I didn't realize the magnitude of just how much. When she began to speak again, I didn't move, transfixed by what she might reveal.

"We had a fireplace in the living room of the house I grew up in. My parents often had a fire on the colder nights. And I'd sit in front of it in a little rocking chair my grandmother gave me and just watch the fire. Over time, I realized I could do things with it—make it rise and fall, or make it move toward a log to make it catch. I'd try to get my parents' attention, the way kids do—'Look at me!' I'd say and show them how I could make the fire move.

"At first they didn't believe me. But when they realized I was telling the truth, they got scared. After I went to bed, I'd overhear them arguing about it. What they were going to do. Should they tell someone? A psychologist, maybe? Or someone specializing in the supernatural? But then, they thought it was too much for a kid. They tried to ignore it and hoped it would go away."

"But Maya, didn't they see that what you have is a gift?" Mother asked. "When you're given such abilities, you should cultivate them, not suppress them."

She shot a quick look at me. I scowled back at her in return. Mother and I had different feelings about my abilities. If she had to live with it for one day, I was sure she'd change her tune.

Maya answered. "I guess they just wanted me to lead a normal life. When you're a kid, being *special* really isn't so special. You want to be like everyone else."

Ah, what I'd craved my entire life. To be normal, like everyone else. Maya understood.

"What happened as you grew up?" Mother asked.

"My abilities didn't go away as my parents had hoped. They learned to live with it and not fear it after a while, I think. Kind of like it just being a quirk of someone in your family. But when I became a teenager, I started playing with it more. Doing tricks in the fireplace. They'd tell me to stop showing off." She grinned. "I guess it was kind of flashy."

"Flashy?" I repeated. "It's rather amazing, I would think. And what about now? You're a firefighter. That would be kind of an odd coincidence."

She smiled in a way that made my inner core melt. At that moment, I wanted to scoop her up and find someplace quiet where we could be alone. Somewhere we could continue exploring each other like we had earlier where I had only just started getting to know her body. There was so much more I wanted to know about her—her personality, her likes, and her body and desires. But that would have to wait because right now I wanted to hear the rest of Maya's story.

I smiled back at her in a way I hoped would cause the same effect she had on me.

"Yes, Tristan, it would," she agreed, raising one eyebrow.

Why was she doing this to me? Didn't she know how hard it was to concentrate when I simply wanted to pounce on her? We were at my parents' house for crying out loud, nobody wants to think about sex around their parents, but that promising smile was overwhelming enough to take over all my senses.

Maya ran her fingers through her straight black hair. I watched her hands. With a gentle touch, she'd stroked my body with them last night. When would she touch me like that again?

She continued, "I use this skill I have with fire—or whatever it is that I have with it—to kind of perceive where the fire is going, what it's going to do. If there's going to be a big blowout with walls coming down or something like that, I sense it a moment before it happens. It's not enough to stop it, but it's enough to sometimes get people out of the way."

"Fascinating," I said so softly I wasn't sure if she heard me. A sort of premonition for where fire was heading. Was it foresight? Or a connection with fire? Either way, it was something I didn't understand, nor did I think anyone in my family had ever experienced.

"But sometimes, sometimes I can," Maya said.

"Can what, my dear?" Mother asked. I noticed that she was barely moving, as entranced by Maya's description of her connection with fire as I was. If not more so.

"Sometimes I can control it," Maya said. "The fire. When it's small enough and not flaming out of control, I can sort of —guide it. Calm it or slow it down. It may sound crazy, but it's true. It works."

"How does it work?" I asked.

"I'm not sure I can explain it. I've never told anyone before besides my parents, you know. And I only told them so much because they didn't want to encourage it, like I explained." She hesitated. "One time I was on a call for a house fire. The fire was in the kitchen and I was the first one to enter the room. The fire was spreading across the kitchen walls right toward a pan filled with grease on the stove. I tried to extinguish it, but it was moving too quickly. If it hit the grease, the situation would get a whole lot worse in an instant. But my attempt to put out the fire with the hose was only so effective. So instead I used my mind to communicate with it. I tried to tell it to go in the opposite direction. Not out loud like I'm talking to you now, but in my head. I spoke to it gently and willed it to go away from the stove."

When she paused, I realized I'd stopped breathing as I

listened to Maya's story. I sat back and resumed normal breathing patterns and waited for her to continue. Mother must have been doing the same thing since she readjusted in her chair and then focused intently on Maya again.

Maya continued. "Believe it or not, the fire started moving in the other direction. And it had slowed down. It defied all logic from what I had experienced with house fires in the past. But now, it was under control somewhat so when other firefighters came in, we were able to extinguish the flames."

"Amazing," I whispered.

She truly was one-of-a-kind. Not just with her special glow, but she was powerful in her own right. And in bed, forget it, I couldn't think about that now and get an erection in front of my parents.

My mother started to speak, but then stopped. Maya noticed as well and encouraged her to continue. "Isabella, would you like to ask me something?"

Mother hesitated, something I'd rarely seen in someone as confident as she was. Then she said, "I was just wondering —if it wouldn't bother you—if you could show us. You know —what you can do with fire."

Maya's face darkened for a moment. Oh no, we'd gone too far. Being treated like a freak was something I had experienced and I was sure she didn't find it welcoming.

"Mother, I don't think that's appropriate. This is not a circus; she shouldn't be asked to perform."

Maya surprised me by saying, "No, it's okay, Tristan. I know it's meant well. It's just not something I show people often, you know? Give me a moment to think, clear my head."

Our eyes met. I nodded in understanding.

She looked around. "This fire pit out here will work just fine," she said.

She then gathered some pieces of wood and small twigs for kindling and put them in the fire pit. "I left my purse inside. There's a lighter in there."

"There's one in here," Mother said, reaching into a basket and handed over a lighter for the grill.

Maya lit a small fire in the pit in seconds. Then she sat back.

"Ready for the freak show?" she asked. She didn't wait for an answer, but focused her gaze onto the tiny flames. "I'm going to make it rise now, double in size."

The flames rose; indeed, they did double in size. And it happened so gradually, as if it took no effort on her part.

"Oh my God," Mother said.

"That's nothing, really," Maya said, brushing it off. "Now I'm going to make it rise more and move. Watch it move steadily from right to left, right to left."

I watched the fire, entranced, as it did exactly as she said, moving sinuously from one direction to another as if it were dancing.

"Brilliant!" Mother squealed, clapping her hands in delight.

"And now, a funnel," Maya said.

The fire then swirled counter-clockwise; indeed, it did appear to take a funnel form. I'd never seen anything like it.

Maya looked at me and giggled. "It's not that amazing, Tristan. Your mouth is hanging wide open."

Quickly closing my mouth, I recovered my wits. "What about the night of the fire at Vamps? What happened that night?"

A furrow line appeared between her brows. "There was only so much I could do that night. The explosion spread from one wall through the club."

"You must have done something," I said. "Nobody was killed."

"I did whatever I could to will the fire to slow it down, calm it, direct it away from the bar where it was heading. If it reached the alcohol, it would accelerate. It wasn't a small kitchen fire, though, so I don't know how effective I was."

"I think you had to have been pretty influential that night in saving people's lives. And possibly in keeping the fire from progressing. The damage was bad, but it could have been worse. Most of the building was untouched."

She shrugged.

"So maybe I have to thank you for saving what was to become my new business. The building was salvageable. I got it for a steal. It was a quick sale since the owner had business to tend to abroad and said he couldn't oversee the renovations when they rebuilt the club."

Maya clicked her tongue on the roof of her mouth.

"What is it?" I asked.

"Nothing. Go on."

I took her hand in mine. "Thank you, Maya. For everything."

When I saw the earnest look in her blue eyes, she left me speechless.

"My pleasure. It changed my life for the better, too."

I was hoping that she meant by meeting me. After searching my brain for an appropriate response, all I could think of were words about fate and destiny, too heavy for the moment, especially in front of Mother.

As if on cue, Mother spoke. "You have an affinity for fire, Maya. One of the four elements. That's an ancient power. One we don't see much anymore."

"Would that explain her light?" I asked.

Mother thought for a moment. "Perhaps it would." She furrowed her brow as she looked out onto her gardens. "There is so much magical history with light versus darkness.

The fact that you two were brought together shouldn't be ignored."

I shifted in my chair and noticed as Maya suddenly feigned interest in a lock of her black hair.

Mother naturally ignored our obvious discomfort, as always thinking of the bigger magical picture.

"Tristan, Maya must be the light to counter the darkness."

"Mother, what are you talking about? We just met. You're going to scare Maya away!"

Maya gave me a gentle smile. "It's okay, Tristan. I'd like to hear more."

No woman had shown me such compassion before. Any other woman I had bedded would surely have bolted on hearing anything so heavy. I wanted to mouth *Thank you*, but instead made a mental note to thank her later.

"I don't know," Mother said. "But light and darkness are opposites, like yin and yang. They need balance. One shouldn't exist without the other."

"So, you're saying we might balance each other out?" Maya asked.

"I'm saying you two need to work together to figure it out."

Maya's gaze met mine, echoing my unspoken question.

How would we do that?

CHAPTER 7

M*aya*
Isabella asked Tristan to excuse us so we could have some time for "girl talk" in the courtyard. When Tristan went to find his father, my gaze wandered to a garden of autumn flowers the color of sunsets.

I didn't know how I felt about this, being left with a woman who descended from a long line of witches. She was attuned to the Earth and seemed so sure in her skin. And now, she knew my secret.

Plus, she was the mother of the hot guy I started sleeping with, with whom I might have some secret destiny.

"Thank you, Maya, for staying to chat."

"What did you want to talk about?"

She tapped her finger on the table as if debating what to say next. "Some friends and I—we meet here every month during the full moon. Perhaps you'd like to join us one day."

"Are they—" I didn't want to come out and say witches as it sounded weird coming out of my mouth. Would it be offensive? Who knew the PC terms in their world? I searched for a suitable word. "Gifted? Like you?"

She nodded.

"Is it—a coven?"

"We call it a circle," she clarified. She tapped her fingers again. "I hope you don't take this the wrong way, but I think you have much potential."

"For what?"

"To tap into your gifts. And maybe for a more selfish reason—to help my son."

"Oh. Um. I don't know what to say. I mean, this is all coming on very quickly. I don't even know how to process everything yet."

"Wait right here, please," Isabella said. "I'll be right back." She went inside for a moment and came back with an ornate carved wooden box. When she opened it, I saw a colorful set of cards set against maroon velvet lining.

"Would you let me do a reading?"

"What kind of reading?" I asked.

"Just some Tarot cards. Have you ever had them read for you?"

"No." I leaned forward. "Sure, why not."

Isabella shuffled the cards and explained how she'd be reading in the Celtic Cross fashion. She had me concentrate on whatever problem or concern I had, and then pick a number of cards. I did. My thoughts turned through random thoughts, but most drifted to what she'd uncover about my ability with fire—or any sort of future with Tristan.

She laid them out for past, present, future, hopes, obstacles and so on. Each time she turned over a card, she said a few words on each, but she didn't get animated until the end.

"The Star. Another major arcana. You've been feeling the lack of a sense of meaning in your life. And the lack of someone special. You desire more."

Heat suffused my cheeks. The reading had quickly turned personal.

"You'll find a connection with someone special, something so deep that it will seem your tie is unbreakable. However, you will be hurt, forced into estrangement."

What the—? "By the same person?"

She shook her head. "It's unclear. You will come through and learn much about yourself."

I shook my head. "What does this mean? A special connection, estrangement, new ability? I'm confused."

Isabella put down the cards and looked at me. "Be true to yourself and follow your path. Only then will you get what you desire."

I was speechless, a rare moment. Then, trying to lift the mood, I laughed. "Whoa, that was intense."

"Need a moment to yourself?" she asked.

"No, I'm fine." I needed to direct the attention away from me. "So, Isabella, are you psychic? Can you see the future?"

She smiled warmly. "I just help people understand what's troubling them, maybe help them uncover their true desires. I lead them toward the path they want to go down."

"Oh," I said, not knowing what I should say. "Is there anything else you wanted to talk to me about?"

Isabella sat back in her chair. "Perhaps I shouldn't be telling you this as Tristan might get upset. He's so protective of his privacy."

I braced myself for what was coming. What did she want to tell me?

"You're the first woman he's ever brought home. It's such a pleasure to meet you. You seem to have brought a change on him, a lightness, and I don't mean anything to do with the light he sees around you. I mean a lightness to his soul. A contrast to all the weight he feels he's carrying on his shoulders."

"Thank you. We haven't known each other long, but I'm glad to be of any help to whatever burden he feels."

"That's the thing, Maya," Isabella said. "Tristan's gift—he believes it's a curse because he can't live a normal life. And maybe he's right. But for any curse, there's a way to lift it. I don't believe it's a curse, though. It must be a gift. He must have been given those abilities for a reason. And if he learns to understand them and develop them, he'll find peace. Maybe even happiness."

I realized I tilted my head, which I often did unconsciously when thinking. "What do you think the reason might be?"

"I believe that he was born to be a healer. My grandfather —Tristan's great-grandfather—had an ability to heal people. I don't know how he did it, but the stories I heard were that he could see things in people the rest of us couldn't. And whatever he saw in them gave him insight on how to heal them. Tristan must have inherited this gift. His abilities to sense darkness and sadness in people must be connecting to being able to heal that sadness."

I thought about it. "That would make sense. But Tristan hasn't described what he sees as positive. In fact, they sound rather terrifying."

Isabella leaned back and smiled. "That's where I think you come in. I believe in destiny," she said. "Maybe you've come into Tristan's life for a reason."

Whoa, that was a lot to process. As of yesterday morning, I was just a firefighter who had a few harmless fantasies about some hot guy she saw in a club. Okay, maybe I had my weird little fire thing, but still, I was used to that. Now I'm some sort of partner in destiny with a guy I just met? I'd admit I felt some sort of connection to him, but to commit to work on something that intense together?

"I don't know, Isabella. That seems a little out there to me."

"I can understand that," she said. "Just do one thing for me, please. Be open to it. Don't shut the idea out completely."

Something about this woman, almost a complete stranger, believing I was capable of so much made me want to believe it myself. Maybe I didn't think I hooked up with Tristan for anything more than the hottest sex of my life. But that didn't mean I couldn't be open to the possibility that we could be more. Who knew? Maybe we could sort of help each other out somewhat? Isn't that what people in healthy relationships do—encourage each other to be the best person they can be? And why wouldn't I want to help him? My career was devoted to helping people, mostly complete strangers. He'd moved beyond that characterization to an inner intimate circle. Of one.

"I can do that," I said.

Tristan

I sat with my father on Adirondack chairs on the deck, near his grill and smoker. We each had a glass of iced tea.

"I don't know what it is about Maya," I admitted. "But it's as if I'm under a spell."

My father chuckled. "That's what happens."

With a furrow of my brows, I asked, "When what happens?"

"When you find the right one." His eyes twinkled.

I leaned forward in the Adirondack chair. "But how do you know it's not just—lust? Or infatuation?"

He shrugged, staring out at the trees. "You figure it out eventually."

I exhaled. "It's not easy."

"No, it isn't."

"I don't know. It's all moving so fast. I'm crazy about her, but I'm freaked out too. I don't know if I'm ready for a—relationship."

"*That* happens too."

"Why? Because of my abilities?"

He shook his head. "No, because you're a guy. We can screw things up. Sometimes in a stupid way."

"Tell me about it."

My father stood up. "I'm going to get a refill. Need anything?"

I looked at my still-full glass. "No, thanks." I rose too. "I'll go see what they're up to."

Maya

When Tristan walked into the courtyard I was pulled back to the here and now.

"Is it safe to come back?" he asked.

"Yes, come on in, Tristan." His mother stood and said, "I better go find Eric. We're meeting some friends later. But you two should stay. The house is yours for the evening." Then as if remembering something, Isabella said, "Hold on, I have something for you, Maya." She returned in a moment with a necklace—a gold oval with an S carved on it. "Would you wear this talisman, please? It's for protection. It's something our family creates for people we want to protect."

I ran my finger over the smooth metal, running my finger over the carved S, presumably for Stone. Touched, as I just met this woman, I could only say, "Thank you."

"If I were to bet," Tristan said, "I'd say Maya is the protectress. Protecting those around her."

Isabella nodded slowly as if considering that idea. Then she said, "Tristan's talisman is silver. For healing. Yours is made of copper, for all-around protection and well-being. Focus on it from time to time. It has been consecrated in a circle. But from now on, its energy, its effectiveness, comes from within, from you."

My mouth had fallen open and I snapped it shut. I never

would have imagined a family who would accept me without judgment after knowing my affinity with fire. My family considered it a flaw, which they'd tried to ignore. The Stones embraced it as if it were a gift to be nurtured.

"I will," I said, putting it on with that solemn promise.

After we said goodbye and Tristan's parents left, we walked back into the garden.

"Has my mother grilled you to death?"

"Ah ha. She has a way of coaxing the most hidden secrets out of someone. You know I've never told anyone outside of my family about the fire thing before."

"She has a way of doing that to people. Part of her charm, I suppose."

I reflected on that. In the short time we'd met, I shared my deepest, darkest secrets. She also shared her hopes for her son and how she believed I might be key. She believed in him. She believed in me. It was rare to meet someone to believe in you these days, let alone trust you so soon in this cynical world.

She left quite the impression on me. I wondered if she had that effect on everyone she met.

Tristan must have been deep in his own thoughts because he arrested his pace suddenly to look at me. "I'm glad you trusted us enough to share it. I'm glad you can trust me."

Trust. That must be the theme of the day.

"Let's not count our chickens before they hatch," I teased. "I mean, you are still a weirdo and all."

"And so are you, my dear." He pulled me to his chest and searched my eyes. "Honestly, you don't think we're too —out there?"

"I thought your parents were lovely. Is your Dad, you know, like you?"

"Witchcraft is strong in Dad's family, but he doesn't seem

to have inherited any of the—sensitivities. Not like Mom being a medium and all."

I snapped my head back on hearing that revelation. "Come again now?" I shook my head. "She just read my Tarot cards."

"She didn't mention how she can communicate with the dead?"

"Um—no. I think I would've remembered that."

"She was probably too fascinated with you. Same as me. Only my thoughts are far more lascivious. I find you even more alluring now that I know you won't judge me as much as I feared."

Without any warning, he bent down to kiss my lips and enclose me in a fierce embrace. My body instantly responded as I melted into his arms and my lips met his with equal enthusiasm.

"How do you set me on fire so quickly?" I asked in between kisses.

He pushed me against the wall of his parents' house. "You're the one who controls the fire, Maya. And you have it raging inside me right now."

I lifted one leg and he caressed me from my ankle toward my thigh. Then he grabbed my other leg and lifted me up, holding me against the wall. My flowing black skirt, which I earlier thought was appropriate for meeting my man's parents, seemed much more suggestive as it hiked up near the tops of my thighs.

"Here? What if the neighbors see?" I asked.

"That just makes it all the hotter," he replied.

He glanced around the neighboring houses. "It's dark out. They'd only see shadows. Besides, I don't see any peeping Toms looking for a free show right now."

When he pressed himself against me, I moaned. The

whole thing felt so wrong—and of course, so right. All the buildup from the night in the cemetery and then outside the building came rushing back. He was right—the prospect of getting caught made it all the hotter.

Pinning me against the wall with his weight, he managed to pull my panties down and slide them off one leg and then the other.

"You're quite deft with your hands," I said.

"I haven't even gotten started." He reached under my skirt and touched me and I realized just how skilled he actually was with his hands. How he managed to pin me against the wall, touch me, and kiss me was a mystery. But he was so tall and muscular, my weight was probably nothing to him.

"Oh yes," I assented. "You're right. This is perfect. Fuck me now before I come right here."

"Don't hold back. Go ahead."

He touched me more intensely, putting pressure on just the right spot.

Oh yeah, there.

I glanced at all the bright reds in the garden while the intensity heightened, and then exploded.

"Oh God!" I cried.

"Yeah. Fuck yeah."

Still dazed by my climax, I was surprised when he put me on my feet.

"Hold on, beautiful." He unzipped his pants and pulled them down just far enough to release his cock. "I want to fuck you up against this wall."

I looked around quickly to make sure no strangers had wandered into the garden and were watching our little performance. "Hell, yes."

"And I want to see these." He unbuttoned my blouse and undid my bra.

I looked down and saw my pale breasts shining in the moonlight. Tristan was right about it being dark out, but the moon was clearly putting the spotlight on us if my breasts were any indication of the scene. If anyone was looking— well, now they'd see a lot.

What was Tristan doing to me? All this outdoor recreation was new to me—and so exhilarating.

He fished out a condom from his pocket and rolled it over his cock. Then he picked me up again and I wrapped my arms around his neck. Somehow he managed to slide inside me as he held me against the wall. As it stretched me, I gasped. Although we had sex the night before, the full feeling of him inside me was still a new sensation. And it had been so long since I'd wanted someone this badly.

Had I *ever* wanted anyone this badly?

I met his rhythm and worked myself against him as the friction rose. Oh God, I was going to come again so soon.

"Damn, Tristan. You know how to push just the right buttons."

Right there.

Oh. My. God.

My world intensified and exploded once again, but different this time with him inside me.

"That was amazing," I said.

He let me down gently so I didn't scrape myself against the house.

"Now lie down," I said. "I'm not done with you yet."

"Oh, firecracker, I hope you mean that. Because I don't want you to be done with me for a long time."

"We can't fool around out here all night. Your parents will be back at some point."

"I meant more than that."

Knowing full well what he meant, I said, "Don't worry. Let me take care of you."

He lay down on the grass and I climbed on top of him, easing myself down over him.

"You feel so good inside me," I said as the tempo rose. "So fucking good I can hardly take it."

"I know," he said. He slid his hands under my shirt to feel my breasts. "Makes me wish I met you a long time ago."

This time when the intensity rose, his excitement rose with mine as he drove into me with increasingly deep thrusts. When I called out his name and exploded all over him, he grabbed my hips and pumped deep inside me, releasing within me.

I collapsed onto his chest. We lay there panting for a few minutes, our limbs entwined around each other on the cool grass, as we reveled in the afterglow.

After our breathing levels returned to normal, he said, "Hey Maya, I want to show you something inside."

I propped myself up to glance at his face. "I *think* you just showed me something quite impressive."

"Ha! Well, thank you. I meant something to cool off." His grin was so mischievous, like a little boy.

"What is it?"

"Come with me." He rolled me off him, removed the condom, and dressed.

I readjusted my clothing and followed him inside. After he shed evidence of our tryst by flushing the condom, he led me down the hall. We entered a pantry where a big freezer took up much of the space.

"You see this freezer. My parents have quite a sweet tooth. Plenty of ice cream in here."

"Ooh, I wasn't expecting that, but that's awesome. I'm eight thousand degrees right now."

He opened the lid. "Look inside. All those flavors."

My mouth salivated. What could be better than hot

outdoor sex than a cool bowl of ice cream? "You frickin' rock, Tristan." I kissed him.

"Let's mix and match," he said, grabbing some sundae glasses. "And maybe if you're good," he added with a wicked grin, "I'll lick some off of you."

CHAPTER 8

T*ristan*

Nights with Maya flew by. But her long shifts at the firehouse were torture. She'd work a 24-hour shift and then crash, catching up on sleep. I waited for her, rather impatiently, and glanced at the clock far too often. To distract myself from missing her, I worked on business matters in my office in the same building as my loft or in my lab beneath the club.

On her next free evening, I asked her to meet me at Vamps.

She wore a blue cotton dress that matched her eyes and had buttons all down the front. Perfect for a casual day at the beach. Or a naughty night. Blood rushed into my cock as I thought about unbuttoning them, one by one.

But that wasn't why I invited her here. We could have fooled around in my loft. I wanted to show her something. I led her downstairs, but then hesitated on the stairwell.

She sensed my hesitation. "What's wrong?"

"This is my secret space."

She looked at me with such a naughty grin that I instantly hardened. "I can keep a secret."

When we entered the library, she ran her fingers down the spines of some leather books. "What a collection."

"My favorites."

"You collect books?"

"Books have been my companions for as long as I can remember. And they're filled with people who are different, outcasts. Without them, my life would have been a whole lot lonelier."

"No friends growing up?"

I shook my head. "Friendships were too difficult for me. It's hard to play games with someone when you're staring in horror at the shadows around them. Besides, I preferred to be alone. Step back. I need to take care of something." I pulled a book forward on the bookcase—*Dante's Inferno*—which triggered a hidden lever underneath it. The bookcase twisted to the side.

"Splendid," she shrieked. "It's as if we're in *Clue*. I love that game!"

"I love games, too. But spicier ones than board games."

"I'm all ears," she said.

"I'll keep that in mind. Now I want to show you some other things."

Her eyes widened as my lab was revealed by the moving bookcase. "May I?"

"Please." I gestured for her to go on in.

She entered the lab and moved along one shelf after another. "So many bottles and jars. So many books. What is this? What do you *do* in here?"

"Experiment. Make things, brew potions."

"Potions? Like what?"

"Mostly I've been trying to find a cure to my curse."

She looked at me with such concern in her eyes that I was

momentarily disarmed. I appreciated how much this woman might actually care for me. Not just as a lover, but as a person.

"I'm touched that you invited me in here. And I'm honored that you trust me with your secret."

For a moment, I was at a loss for words. When I found my voice, I said, "It's cathartic being able to share it with someone. My mother has been on my case about being too isolated for years. Now I'm starting to understand why."

"You know something, Tristan? Maybe your mother is right about the other thing as well. Perhaps we did meet for a reason."

I had to tease to lighten the serious tone that dominated the conversation. "Hot sex?"

She laughed in surprise at first, but then returned a coquettish gaze. "Naturally. But there could be something more. The way you see me in some light, my thing with fire. I don't know, but maybe there's something to it."

"Okay, maybe there is," I conceded. "How in the hell would we even go about figuring it out?"

She scanned the jars on the shelf again. "No freakin' clue. I don't even know what the heck you have going on down here."

"I know what you have going on down there," I said, giving her a lascivious look. "And I love it."

"You're incorrigible, aren't you, Mr. Stone?" she said. "I guess you have one thing on your mind right now. Maybe we should try for some erotic inspiration?"

"My favorite kind." I moved in to pull her close. Gazing into those sparkling eyes again, I lost myself in them. And when she leaned in to kiss me, I never wanted to be found.

We kissed standing up in the middle of the lab, but then made our way back to the velvet-covered sofa as if in some sort of sensual dance. I pressed myself on top of her as I kissed her neck.

"Experiments," she said. I looked up to see her eyes scanning the shelves again.

"Shh. The only experimentation I want to do right now is on your body."

"Ooh, I like the sound of that. Consider me a willing participant."

"Hold on a sec." I hurried to open some drawers to see what I had on hand. When I found some old scarves, I turned back. "Why don't we start with these?"

"What on earth would we do with that?" Her eyes glimmered with a flirtatious glint.

"Close your eyes."

She hesitated, but then closed them. I thumbed through the scarves to find the softest one and picked a blue silk scarf. I covered her eyes and she lifted her head so I could reach back and tie it behind her.

Having her eyes covered helped steel me for my next step. If she were watching me with those fiery eyes, I might have relented on my plan, and just bent her over the end of the sofa to take her right then.

Her lips parted and I bent down to cover them with my own. "Relax." When she exhaled, I added, "Trust me."

Maya

I'd never been blindfolded before other than playing Pin the Tail on the Donkey. Whenever a past lover had suggested it, I flat-out said no. It involved a level of trust that I simply did not feel. But when Tristan did it, my hesitation was only momentary.

The silk felt cool and satiny on my skin. And the sensation of being blindfolded heightened all my other senses. My God, this was intense.

Every nerve in my body was alert, wondering and waiting to see what he'd do next.

His footsteps softened. He was walking away. Where was he going?

My question was answered when I heard music fill the room. Someone crooning, "You never really know" in a rich, seductive voice. I wondered who was singing and wanted to ask, but my anticipation for what would happen next drowned out my curiosity.

He breathed on my wrist before he kissed me there. He then raised my hand and entwined my arm with a satiny fabric.

"What are you doing?" I whispered.

"Shh. Just wait. If something bothers you too much, just tell me to stop."

His lips moved up my arm to my neck. My body heated up so quickly. Just the anticipation of his next move set my skin on fire.

"You're wearing the amulet."

"Uh-huh. I love it."

His lips moved down above my breasts. His finger played with the buttons. I'd purposely left the top one undone to give a hint of skin while leaving something to the imagination.

When he unfastened the first button, I exhaled, unaware that I'd been holding my breath. He kissed me where he had uncovered the skin and moved on to the next button. When he unfastened that button and kissed me there, my body hungrily anticipated the next button as he moved down the front of my body.

Oh, this was sweet, slow torture.

By the time he reached my navel, I was writhing in anticipation beneath him. Then his warm breath over my panties.

I swore I would shatter just from that. That's how ready I was. Waiting for more.

Is he going to continue this sweet torment with the rest of my clothing? Damn, why didn't I go commando tonight?

His lips were on my inner thighs as he unfastened the last two buttons. My body arched, desperate for more.

My dress fully open now, I lay there blindfolded in just my royal-blue lace bra and panties. When he whispered, "Stunning," I was glad I chose to wear undergarments after all.

"Scoot up for a sec. I want to get this dress off you."

I did what I was told and he pulled the dress off my arms and out from under me.

"I want to fuck you so badly right now," he said.

"Then do it," I pleaded.

"No. Wait. Trust me. It'll be worth it."

He reached behind me and unfastened my bra, pulling it off me, and let out a low groan. "Beautiful," he murmured.

He inched his fingers inside the waistline of my panties and he pulled them down. I raised my hips to aid him and then lay back down, aware I was fully naked and blindfolded.

The song ended, replaced by another with a mounting tempo. I recognized it. *The Hunter's Prelude* from the *Bram Stoker's Dracula* soundtrack. As the tempo rose, my anticipation grew as well. What was he going to do next?

My question was soon answered when he took my already bound wrist and lifted the other. He tied them together above my head and let them rest behind me on the end of the sofa.

Oh God, he's tying me up. Blindfolded. Tied up. Never done this before. The wait is agony.

Then Tristan's mouth was on my index finger, sucking it in and out. His tongue flicked over my finger, filling me with anticipation. And then with one last suck, he moved away.

His kisses moved down my arms, then to my thighs. Down, down he kissed along my legs. Down to my ankles. I guessed what was coming next. Another scarf.

As if reading my mind, he said, "I'm leaving your legs untied this time. I want them spread open." He eased my legs apart. "Wider. I want to see all of you."

Being so naked while I couldn't see any of it had me panting again.

Something light tickled my ankle. What was it? It moved up my leg, leaving a trail of sensation in its wake. Was it a feather?

Yes, it had to be. He brushed me with it, up, up, up to my breasts. Over them. My nipples hardened. And then his tongue was licking and suckling one, while his hand caressed my other breast. He moved his mouth to the other breast while I barely breathed, so caught up in my longing.

"Hold on," he whispered.

"What?" I gasped. No. He couldn't leave me waiting like this.

After a few agonizing seconds, I heard a scratchy sort of noise and then smelled the sulfur of a match.

"It's okay. I'm just lighting a candle," he said.

"For what?"

"Candlelight. And maybe—you."

"Oh. Are you going to…"

"Do you want me to?"

A part of me screamed no. Flame. Pain. No way.

Another part, the part of me that was already consumed by flames at this point, took over. I nodded.

"What was that?" Tristan teased.

"Ye-yes."

"Are you ready?"

I braced myself for heat, pain. But where?

Heat concentrated in my inner thighs as I felt the flame move closer.

Put it out!

No, wait. Wait for it. See what happens.

In the next second, pain scorched my inner thigh. And then the other one. The intensity of the sensation was underscored by the music pummeling all around us.

"Oww," I cried out.

The candle wax must have hardened instantly because Tristan pulled it off my skin. The pain was instantly replaced by coolness. A water bottle? And then warm, soft lips.

Holy crap, this is too much. I'm going to explode any second.

"Good girl," he whispered. "Are you okay?"

"Uh-huh," I managed to squeak out and nodded.

The next song was *Paralyzer*, one I recognized from the club, the night I met Tristan.

"This song played the night I fell for you."

"Oh." I sighed.

"I'm going to put something on you now. Something warm. Spread your legs."

"What is it?" I asked, already burning with longing down there.

"Just a tasty little potion. Don't worry, you'll like it."

The potion felt cool when he poured it onto me and I squealed. But then his breath only an inch away warmed it up.

Oh, this was heaven. Exquisite torture and heaven all at once.

And then finally, his tongue was on me. I wanted to reach down and feel his hair, but my wrists were tied.

The muscles in my thighs tightened as my excitement rose. He tortured and rewarded me with his artful tongue and then entered me with skillful fingers.

And then his fingers were replaced by something bigger

and firmer. I heard the vibrations the moment before I felt it inside me. He played with me so artfully, as if he knew exactly what my body needed next.

It didn't take long for the tempo to rise and I lifted my lower body to get closer, closer still, before I exploded all around him in blissful release. Incoherent words mingled with moans escaped from my lips.

When fabric rustled, I pictured him undressing.

"Hurry," I managed to say.

"Okay, baby. One sec."

The seconds I waited while he ripped open a package and put on a condom were agonizing. When I finally felt the head of his cock tease me, I said, "Now. Please. Now."

I was so wet that he eased right inside me, despite me tightening reflexively around him. His thick cock filled me so much I could barely take it.

But I wanted it. More of it. So, I rose against him and met each one of his thrusts. The friction intensified and I climbed, climbed—but then he stopped.

"Not yet. I'm going to come too quickly like this. You feel too good. But I want to do something else first."

He untied me so I had free use of my hands and he turned me around so I was headfirst over the armrest of the sofa. When he drove into me again, slamming in from behind, I grabbed onto the armrest and braced myself for more.

From this angle, the penetration was so intense. He held on to my shoulders for leverage, which also kept me from falling over the edge. Each time his cock rammed into me, I cried out.

Heat rose within me again with the increasing friction. The orgasm that was building threatened to overcome me. Each time he pummeled into me shot me closer to my peak. Building, rising, shooting higher…

When I crashed over the edge, the quakes were so intense

that I fell forward, gripping the armrest. Tristan pulled me back up, grasping my shoulders and pumped me so hard that I knew he was about to come. His cock throbbed deep inside me as he slammed into me and exploded.

After a few heart-pounding seconds, he kissed my shoulder and lightly bit it. Then, he collapsed over the armrest with me.

"Holy shit," I said.

"That was incredible."

We maneuvered into upright positions on the sofa and Tristan took the blindfold off me.

"I've never done that before," I admitted, fingering the blue silk.

"Did you like it?"

"What do *you* think?"

"You seemed mighty interested."

A naughty vixen hiding inside me took over. "Next time it's my turn to play with you." I ran the scarf over his eyes to make my meaning clear.

When I heard Tristan's quick inhale, I said, "I take that as a yes."

At the start of my shift the next day, I cleaned and tested equipment in the firehouse, as per our usual daily checklist.

"Someone's really chipper this morning," one of the junior guys said.

"I know that smile. Someone got laid last night," Rick Muller said in a sing-songy voice.

A confirmed bachelor in his late twenties, he tried to steer any conversation we had to sex. Luckily, he was attracted to a different type of girl so I never had to worry about him making any advances. But if there was an Irish girl, especially with red hair and green eyes, she would have to fight pretty hard to keep him away. Nike with her dark auburn hair had to set him straight a few times. I wouldn't exactly say Rick and I were friends, but we had developed a sort of brother-sister, friendly-competitive banter that made the countless hours working together more entertaining.

I'd worked with Rick forever. Okay, maybe it was just a few years. But when you spend that much time working with a person in close quarters, you get to know each other pretty quickly.

Rick was dead on with his guess, not that I'd admit it to him. I had been replaying the more magical moments from my hot night with Tristan and the blue scarf, which probably resulted in a sappy smile on my face.

"Shut up, butt head," I said. For some reason, most of our terms of endearments for each other involved the mature use of the word *butt*. "I can't be happy about something without you thinking it's related to sex?"

"Can you deny it, Butt Rogers?" he asked.

I bit my lower lip while I thought of a comeback. Coming up short, I flicked some water from my water bottle at him instead.

"Busted," he said. "So, who's the guy?"

"Wouldn't you like to know? I'm not telling you anything."

"Man, I wish Nike was here. I usually could get something out of one of you if I bugged you long enough."

"Yeah, I bet that's the only reason you wish she was here."

"She's hot. I'm not going to deny it."

"And she's long gone."

I wished Nike was there too. Now I was the only female in the firehouse. Which meant I had to bear the full brunt of working with a bunch of nosy guys who were far too interested in my love life.

"What's the deal with this guy?"

"Drop it or I won't cover your shift on Thanksgiving."

"Hey, I have my plane ticket already. You wouldn't."

"Wouldn't I?" I asked, raising an eyebrow.

"Easy. All right, I'll let it go."

Tristan

The next few days with Maya were incredible. Maya listened in fascination as I showed her a cleansing ritual we should start with each time we worked together. We were both determined to understand the reason for our connection. She asked questions about the different color candles and what they were for. She asked to peek into the jars I'd filled with items for my potions.

"Let me guess what's in here—'eyes of newt and toes of frog'?" she asked.

"Very funny. Yes, and I say 'double double toil and trouble' as I stir my cauldron."

"Just teasing, you sexy beast. You know I'm fascinated by this stuff. Ooh, what's this, spices?" She opened the jars to sniff them. "Mmm, cinnamon. Sage?"

I nodded.

"Lavender. And this, I don't know."

"Guarana. From Brazil. Be careful with that—it has much more caffeine than coffee."

She moved on to other jars. "Snakeskin. And some kind of bird feathers."

Maya was intrigued by all the items I'd collected—they were novel to her, but part of everyday life for me. Seeing her examine the contents enchanted me, had me see my work in a new light.

We tried various spells and potions, both for fun and to see what we could do with my condition. The best parts of these sessions were the frequent breaks as we got to know each other better—especially in the bedroom. I'd never had a relationship like this with a woman before. With someone as uninhibited as Maya, the time we spent together intoxicated me. We worked together, laughed together, and then spent the rest of the night exploring each other's bodies. She fascinated me.

Thanksgiving soon came, but Maya had to work. I spent the holiday with my family, as usual. They kept their gatherings small for my benefit, if I was attending. My parents didn't give off the dark shadows like other people did, probably because they were my parents. Who could explain it? Certainly not me.

After she rested, Maya came over the next day. She wore a pinkish-red wig and leather cat suit. So fuckin' hot.

"Oh hell, Maya. What are you doing to me?"

"What?" she asked innocently. "You don't like my outfit?"

"That's the problem. I like it a little too much. Why are you wearing that anyway?"

"I thought we'd go on a little experiment outdoors tonight. Down at the graveyard."

Puzzled, I asked. "And this outfit is necessary how?"

"I love watching reruns of *Alias*. This seems like a perfect opportunity to wear this outfit and perform some reconnaissance."

"Reconnaissance? With a pink wig? In a graveyard?"

"Don't spoil the fun, Tristan," she said. "Lead us on a cleansing ritual and we'll head on down there."

"It will be hard to focus with you in that skintight outfit."

"Then close your eyes."

"Trust me, I'll still be thinking of it."

She smiled decadently. "Tell you what. If you can focus on what we're doing, I'll make it worth your while. You take this outfit off me later. And do whatever you want. Wherever you want."

My eyes bugged out of my head. "I'm focusing, I'm focusing," I said. "Just promise to leave the wig on later."

She raised her pinky finger. "Pinky swear."

Maya

Never did I think I'd plan a task in a graveyard. Yet, that's where Tristan and I ventured later that night.

Tristan stepped before the black wrought iron gates surrounding an old family plot. "What are we going to do here?"

"You asked me if I felt anything in here. Since you see things in here, we should explore that more."

"Okay," he said. The look on his face turned aghast as he looked around. "Do you see them? They're all over tonight."

I looked around the cemetery, but only saw neglected tombstones, old crypts, and moss-covered trees looming over many.

"No, Tristan, I don't," I whispered. "It's okay. Stay calm. Stay focused. They're not going to hurt you."

"Shadows. Everywhere. Lurking through the stones."

"Tristan. Look at me. Not them. Look at my light. Okay, good. Now close your eyes. Hold my hands. Focus. Breathe."

When I thought his terror had subsided, I said, "Open them now."

He looked around. "They're gone."

"Hmm."

"This happened the last time we were here. I looked at you and the darkness disappeared."

"Ah. So, we know what happens," I said. "But why?"

"And what can we do with it?"

Neither one of us had answers. After several moments, I said, "Let's think about that later. While we're here, I can't help but think of the first time we came here, the first time we kissed." Thinking that was true, but I also wanted to relax him, help calm his tormented mind.

A small smile tugged at his lips. "Happiest moment I can remember."

"Hottest moment too." I pressed up against him in my cat suit and kissed him.

A low moan escaped his lips and he pulled me closer. He ran his hands down my back and over my ass, cupping the cheeks.

"God, I love these things," he said, squeezing them.

"It feels good, you doing that," I murmured. "Let's move over there where it's dark, behind that tree." I nodded to the back of the graveyard.

"What do you have in mind, my naughty little vixen?"

"Shhh. Just come along."

I led him behind the tree and kissed him again as I ran my hands down the front of his body, feeling his muscles tighten as I moved. When I cupped his cock, he was already so erect I didn't know how he could stay in those jeans much longer.

I slid down the front of his body, kissing his torso until I kneeled in front of him. I unbuttoned the top button of his pants and undid the zipper, sliding my hand inside to grasp him.

"Here?" he asked, his voice coming out barely a whisper.

"Don't worry, nobody can see us back here."

"But someone might come."

"That someone is you." I slid his jeans and boxers down, freeing his eager, ready cock.

"Oh Maya. What am I going to do with you?"

"You don't have to do anything right now. Just enjoy this."

"I wouldn't—and couldn't—stop this."

I kissed the tip of his cock and he growled. When I licked the shaft, he ran his fingers through my hair.

"Close your eyes," I said. Then I stood and pulled the blue scarf out of my bag. I stood on my tiptoes to wrap it over his eyes and tie it in the back.

"What are you doing?"

"It's my turn to play with you."

LISA CARLISLE

"You're going to blindfold me here? In a graveyard?"

"Shhh." I kneeled back down and took him into my mouth. If the excitement of the forbidden, dangerous aspect of the graveyard excited me, it was likely even more intense without being able to see. Plus, he wouldn't see the shadows.

As I took my time alternating between licking and sucking him, he pumped his hips forward.

"Oh my God. This is incredible. I'm going to come if you keep doing that."

I sucked harder to show I wasn't stopping. He reached back with both arms and grabbed the tree as he arched himself forward one last time, pumping his hot liquid into me and whispering my name.

Tristan

The only exploration we did in the graveyard that night was with each other's bodies. Back at my loft, Maya continued to blow my mind. This time with a striptease to a Danzig song, *She Rides*. I didn't think I'd be able to make it through the song without throwing her on the floor and taking her right there. But she entranced me as she pulled off the leather cat suit ever so slowly, and I didn't dare want to miss a second of it.

"Leave the wig on." I said.

Shadows? Graveyard? What graveyard? She'd distracted me of my earlier torment, and now I couldn't wait for what was yet to come.

She stood naked wearing the pink wig and pointed. "Come get me, tiger."

I jumped out of the seat and carried her to the bed. She squealed with delight until I silenced her with a kiss. The only sounds that followed were her soft pants and cries, which drove me wild, as I buried myself into her.

Sex with her was amazing. It was always amazing. We were a perfect fit.

After we cooled off with limbs tangled around each other, I seared another moment with her to my memory. The blue scarf would never be just some scarf again. And leather cat suits? Purr.

MAYA STAYED OVER MOST NIGHTS. I grew accustomed to her presence. When she was gone, it was as if something was missing.

How did she become such an important part of my life? I was alone for so long and thought I always would be. Holding her in my bed at night comforted me in a way I never knew existed.

Yet, at the same time, a part of me whispered that this happiness was only temporary. It couldn't last forever. I was too dark, too damaged. Unfit as a companion. And Maya was vivacious. She deserved more. Someone who wouldn't hold her back from life.

Pushing reality aside, I focused on now and the time we had. As she sat on the sofa flipping through a magazine, I searched through my music collection.

"Hey Maya, this is your song," I teased as I played one by The Cult.

She looked and turned her head to the side as she listened. "*Fire Woman*? Oh, you're funny." She threw a pillow at me and went to my laptop.

"What are you doing?"

"Getting you back. I'm looking for your song."

"Ha, good luck. I'm one of a kind!"

"That you are." Her eyes raked my body. "Come over here," she said, sauntering to the bed.

Just like that she switched from teasing me to seducing

me. And I responded to the slightest hint of her desire like a Pavlovian dog. No doubt, I was hooked.

Unfortunately, I had to tend to the club and she had to work at the firehouse. Once our duties were done, we met in the lab. We spent the next several days focused on our new hobby—each other.

That and the other reason we had come together. Was there a deeper reason for our connection? And would we ever figure it out?

CHAPTER 9

After a very energetic lovemaking session, we lay panting on my pullout sofa in my lab. She was lying on her stomach and I ran a finger up her spine, tracing the intricate swirls in her tattoo. "Can I ask you something?"

"Sure," she replied. "The tattoo?"

"No. But now that you mention it, yes."

"Just a design I like."

"And the flames?"

"You know my secret."

I nodded.

"What's your question?"

"You know how I see you in light. But deep down I see a darkness in you. As if you're sad."

She bristled.

"Am I making you uncomfortable?"

"No. I just don't know where you're going with it."

"I wonder about it. Often." I propped myself up on one elbow. "Why are you sad deep down? My mind runs wild thinking someone hurt you and it makes me want to destroy them."

"Settle down, tiger," she said, rolling on her side to face me.

I caught the sight of her breasts and grew aroused again.

"No need to seek and destroy anyone," she said. "I'm no different from anyone else. The usual disappointments in life."

"Like what?"

"Oh, you know. People come, people go. You think they'll be in your life, but they disappear."

"Your birth parents?"

She shrugged. "Maybe. But what do I know about that? I was a baby. It's hard to contemplate a loss of something that was never really there."

"Boyfriend?"

"Perhaps. I've had my heart broken, same as any girl who's ever been a teenager."

"Anyone else?"

She opened her mouth and then closed it.

"Maya?"

"A good friend of mine just vanished from my life not too long ago. I wish she'd just tell me the real reason why."

"What happened?"

"That's the thing. I don't know. We were inseparable—we worked together, hung out together—like sisters, I imagine. I don't know since I don't have any. And then, she disappeared with the previous owner after the fire and has been all cryptic since."

Apparently, I unearthed some feelings she'd buried for a while. She continued her tirade.

"I mean, why can't she just tell me what's going on? Why did she just take off with this guy? Who leaves a decent job, a job she was good at and worked hard to get, for some guy? She had a nice apartment and everything. Sends some moving company to pack her stuff up and put it in storage—

it's crazy. Ugh, it makes me sick. When a strong, confident woman leaves everything to go off for a man, I just *hope* there's a reasonable explanation behind it."

After a significant pause when I thought it was safe to speak, I said, "Maybe there is."

She raised one eyebrow. "Really? What could possibly be so important that you'd run off and leave everything behind?"

She had me there. "I don't know. But from my experience, you should never judge how a person acts or what they've decided unless you've been in their shoes."

She snorted. "Sounds a bit cliché."

"But true. Think about it. Most people think I'm extremely—peculiar. The way I isolate myself. If they knew the reason why, well, maybe they wouldn't be so quick to judge."

She looked sheepish for a moment.

"And you, with your connection to fire. If people knew, they probably wouldn't understand and would just dismiss you as some kind of freak."

She bit her lip. "Yeah, you're right. I shouldn't be so quick to judge. You asked why I was hurt and that's the most recent thing."

"Maybe I shouldn't have pried."

"I'm glad you did. I'd buried it for so long I was starting to grind my teeth at night." Then she gave me a wickedly sinful smile and said, "Bet you thought I was going to say it was some guy."

I opened my mouth and closed it. "Maybe. I didn't know what you'd say."

"Yeah, I know. Jealous much?" she teased and threw a pillow at me and tried to scoot away.

"Oh, you're gonna get it. Get over here you." I grabbed her ankle and pulled her back toward me and over my lap as she squealed. "Feeling naughty, are we? Perhaps a little spanking is in order."

"Oh yes, I need to be punished," she said, looking over her shoulder. "I've been a very *wicked* girl."

That night I spanked her before we made love and I spanked her good. She loved it, shouting out in protest each time, but then readying herself for more. Seeing my red handprints on her fine pale skin shot excitement straight to my cock. I bent her over the end of the sofa again, grabbing her ass as I fucked her from behind.

I could never get tired of this. I could fuck her every day.

But then after she fell asleep in my arms later that night, the doubts started to settle in.

No matter how much I wanted her with me, I had to think of her happiness. She deserved better than me.

I was the wrong man for her.

Maya

I ordered a drink while waiting for Tristan. He'd agreed to meet me upstairs at Vamps for a breather tonight. We'd been hiding out downstairs or in his loft while we experimented in all sorts of fun ways, but now I wanted to get out and dance.

"What have you got there?" a woman asked me, nodding toward my drink.

She was quite attractive, with dark, wavy hair and goth-style makeup. I couldn't help but give her a quick once-over, the way you do when you see a beautiful woman. She was wearing a skintight black outfit that showed every curve.

"It's a Tempting Fate," I said. "It's really good. You should try one."

"I'll have to get that next," she said. "I'm Maddie. Great club, isn't it?"

"Maya," I replied. I wanted to proudly add how my guy

was the owner of the club and how he was the reason this club made such a hot comeback. But I stifled my enthusiasm, wary of being overzealous. "Yes, one of my favorites. It's not just the music and the people, but it's all the little details that make it its own."

"So, Maya, are you here with anyone? Someone as beautiful as you shouldn't be drinking alone."

Was she hitting on me? Or just being polite?

"My boyfriend is meeting me here. He promised me we'd dance tonight. It's been too long."

She laughed. "Men who dance. A rare breed."

I looked around. There were a good number on the dance floor tonight. But then I thought about the other men in my life. Would any of the firefighters I worked with be caught dead on a dance floor, let alone a dance floor like this one? Leather, vinyl, costumes and scantily clad bodies abounded.

Just then, a dark-haired man sporting a Van Dyke snaked an arm around Maddie from behind and kissed her on the cheek.

"Maya, this is my husband Roderick."

"Maya," he said, giving me a nod.

"Nice to meet you."

Maddie said, "Roderick and I host couples parties at our house. Maybe you and your boyfriend would like to join us sometime."

Couples parties? Did she mean no kids allowed? Or was she talking about the more kinky variety with an open-door sex policy?

"Um, what kind of parties do you mean exactly?"

"Oh, no pressure or anything. We just look for some open-minded couples like ourselves who are looking for fun, friendship and, you know—maybe a little more."

The hungry look they both gave me told me all I needed to know about what the little more might mean. And I did not know how I felt about it. Part of me was ready to hightail it out of there. But another part noticed the flush of excitement that shot through my body.

"Umm, I don't know. Maybe. I've never been to anything like that before."

She wrote down her name and number on a scrap of paper. "If you're ever intrigued and want to find out more, just give me a call. Like I said, no pressure."

As they walked away from the bar onto the dance floor, I watched them. He was kind of hot in a Latin lover way. He shook it with style. And she was definitely a head-turner. I tried to picture myself kissing her. Would I like kissing a woman? Would I like to do other things with a woman like her?

Hmm, stuff to ponder while I nursed my drink. What about Tristan? Would he be into this? We did some freaky-ass shit together already. I didn't know how I felt about inviting other people into our sexual play. But, hey, it could be fun...an experimental, open-minded, sensual kind of fun.

Tristan interrupted my fantasy. "Hey, firecracker. How are you?" He kissed me on the lips.

"Fine," I said, remembering where I was. "Now that I have you here and I'm not left to my own devices."

"Yes, we wouldn't want that, would we? You could get into all kinds of trouble."

"Quite true."

I looked at Maddie and Roderick dancing. They were all over each other in an uninhibited way. Maddie glanced over at us and winked at me.

Hmm. Maybe.

I was about to mention the interesting little invitation we'd received when Tristan said, "Come on. I promised you I'd dance. And I'm a man of my word."

A dance with Tristan was not to be missed. "Thanks. I know you hate being around people for too long."

"I'll just keep my eyes on you." He smiled. "Being around other people is easier with you to focus on."

Tristan and I danced to some industrial tracks, but he seemed distracted, maybe sad. Oh so different from the first time we danced when we couldn't keep our eyes or hands off each other. Something was off tonight. What was it?

The DJ slowed it down with The Smith's *How Soon is Now?* One you were sure to hear every week or two.

I caught Maddie's and Roderick's eyes a few times. The way they looked at each other, the way they ran their hands down each other's bodies—they were definitely hot for each other.

And the way they looked at me and Tristan made me think they were hot for us, too.

A couples party? I was about to point them out to Tristan, but when I looked at him, he appeared troubled. What was up with him? He wasn't looking at anything in particular, but staring off.

"What's wrong, Tristan? You seem distant. Is it too much being up here?"

He looked at me with his dark, soulful eyes, now so full of sadness.

"Just close your eyes and hold me," I said. I pressed myself closer to him and he pulled me tight.

"Oh, Maya," he said. "What am I going to do?"

"Don't do anything right now. Just hold me close. Whatever it is, it'll be all right."

Tristan

I spent the next day brooding. I had thought Maya was right, we had to get out of the lab and take a break, but going up to dance with her last night didn't help. As much as I craved touching her and needed her near me, the end was inevitable.

It would be painful. No more than that. Devastating.

I spun the globe in my lab. I could sense the end coming over the last few days. My moods had darkened and I grew ever more frustrated each time one of our experiments failed yet again.

I thought she might lead to the cure, but it hadn't yet happened. And I started to take my frustration out on her. I snapped at Maya a couple of times while we brewed a potion. She looked at me surprised at first and then dished it back. We fought over little things.

She didn't deserve this. My moods, my darkness.

Maybe she wasn't the light to my darkness after all. And I would end up putting out her light. She would be surrounded by shadows just like everyone else.

God, I would hate myself to destroy something so good.

I played music to distract me. But instead, I played a song that just confirmed my self-doubts—a song I often played in such moments— *Creep* by Radiohead.

As I listened to the song, the old haunt came back. I wasn't a good companion for anyone, least of all someone as good as Maya.

She was so fuckin' special. I didn't deserve her.

Maybe we weren't meant to be together after all.

I played the song twice more, both to confirm my doubts about whether I was good enough for her and to confirm how she was so much better than I deserved.

Then I played *Hurt by* Nine Inch Nails. Was there a more despondent song out there?

I would hurt Maya. Eventually. No matter how much I wanted to make her happy and protect her, I would be the one who hurt her in the end. She couldn't live a normal life with someone as fucked up as me. She deserved someone who didn't have such issues.

If I cared for her at all, I had to protect her from anything or anyone who would hurt her. Unfortunately, that was me.

I had to free her from my burdens. And I had to do it tonight.

Maya

After a shitty day at work, I looked forward to seeing my hot guy with the magic hands and sensuous lips. When I arrived in his lab, Tristan didn't rise to embrace me the way he usually did. He was bent over his workbench, head in his hands.

What was going on with him lately? We didn't even have sex last night. Tristan just spooned me and we fell into a somewhat fitful sleep.

"Tristan? You okay?"

"It's not working. We've tried and tried. I've done all kinds of research. And—nothing."

I put my skull-and-crossbones bike messenger bag down on the floor and went over to rub his shoulders. "It's okay. Maybe we'll find something, maybe we won't."

He turned to look at me and his eyes were red. "No, it's not okay. I've been living with this misery for years. And when I met you I had this tiny hope that I could be normal. But that was a mistake. I don't know why, but I'm cursed. And nothing and nobody can change that."

"Whoa, Tristan," I said. "You're flipping out. Have you slept at all? Your eyes are bloodshot as hell."

He shook his head. "How can I sleep? We got so close. And then—nothing."

"Don't give up yet. I don't mind experimenting with new things." I made a play of slowly crawling across the floor to him, kneeling in front of him to make my double meaning clear.

"No, Maya. Enough!" he said, standing up and ignoring my double entendre. "I can't take any more false hope. No more."

Sitting up, I realized this was not going to go anyplace good. "What do you mean no more? No more what?"

He avoided looking at me. "I'm not good for you. I don't know what you ever saw in me. You need someone you can go out with and socialize in public. Someone you can dance with and not have to worry about whether he's seeing things that torment him. You're an outgoing person. Look at me. I hide in a lab all day, staying away from people. You deserve better. You deserve your true match. We shouldn't be together anymore."

I opened my mouth and then closed it, reopened it and closed it again. Where was this coming from? Finally, I found some words and they spewed out in a jumble of confused thoughts that I didn't even have time to censor before they spilled freely from my lips.

"How could you say that? I'm a grown woman who can make an adult decision on who she does or does not want to be with. Who do you think you are, making that decision for me? Don't try to control me!"

"I'm not trying to control you. I'm trying to protect you."

"We all have our things, you know. Stop with the 'poor me' shit. I've had to live with my freakishness my whole life too, and you don't see me hiding away from reality."

"Don't compare your *gift* with my *curse*!"

"Call it whatever the hell you want. It's just words. If you didn't want to be with me, you shouldn't have strung me along all this time!"

"I didn't string you along. I cared about you. I still do."

"You cared about using me to fix your problem. Now that

you think it can't be done, you're casting me aside. Ugh! I believed in you. No, I believed in us. And not just in our stupid cursed abilities. I believed in *us*." I pointed between us.

"Maya, you're not listening to me. I'm doing this because I care about you and I want you to be happy." He threw his hands up. "I can never make you happy. I'm giving you your freedom. Releasing you from any obligation you feel to help me."

"Piss off, Tristan!"

I grabbed my bag and stormed upstairs, back through the club. Too angry to be around anyone, I planned on getting out of there as quickly as possible.

As I pushed my way through the crowd, my limbs tense and lips quivering from anger, I heard *My Time Has Come* by the Twilight Singers come on. I loved this song. The energy from the crowd around me made me rethink my plan to be alone. Maybe I should dance off some steam before I pouted home. What else would I do with all this angry, excess energy anyway?

I threw myself in with the crowd, trying to lose myself among them. Bits of the fight with Tristan replayed over in my mind and I tried to force it away.

One song blended into another one and still I stayed. *How dare he? I can't believe he fucking just broke up with me. How did I not even see that coming? Fuckin' blindsided!*

I took a quick break at the bar to down a couple of shots. Anything to take the edge off the pain right now.

When I went back out on the dance floor, a tall, built, blond guy dressed all in black danced with me. He was exceptionally good-looking—like Eric from *True Blood*—a Nordic god. He wasn't exactly my type, but he was easy on the eyes. When I caught his clear blue eyes, I thought of Tristan's dark soulful ones.

Nevertheless, I danced with him, anything to try to forget

Tristan. When the Nordic god pulled me close, I didn't pull away as I normally would have. Strong arms around me without any emotional entanglement were quite welcome at the moment.

Maybe I should sleep with him to help me forget about this whole shitty night. That would be a start to forget about Tristan? This guy was hot, after all. It wouldn't be that much of a sacrifice.

Tristan

That didn't go as planned. My words came out too frustrated, too harsh. Didn't Maya realize I did it for her sake, not mine?

I tried to focus on a book of spells, but found it hard to concentrate. Maybe if I put on music it would help. The song I chose made me brood even more. *Something I Could Never Have*. Someone I can never have.

Why didn't I listen to upbeat pop songs? Instead I replayed ones that exacerbated my desolation.

Listening to the song was torture. She made it all go away. The darkness. The shadows.

Without her, all was bleak.

I pushed my chair back so quickly, the chair screeched across the floor.

Time to check on the club. Maybe all the darkness upstairs would distract me from her.

Walking up the stairs, I tried to push away the question that nagged incessantly at the back of my mind:

What have I done?

As I walked around the perimeter, nothing seemed amiss. The usual shadows. And then—the light. *Her* light.

Dammit—she was here. What was she still doing here? Did she stay here to torment me?

I clenched my hands. Who the hell was she dancing with?

As I watched this man paw Maya, pressing against her body, my heart pumped with fury.

How could she do this to me?

I clenched my hands into fists and pushed my way through the crowd to them.

I grabbed her shoulder. "What the hell are you doing?"

Her mouth dropped halfway before she recovered. "It should be obvious. I'm dancing."

"Why are you dancing *here* and *now?*"

"Because I *want to*."

"This is not cool, Maya, and you know it."

She spun out of her partner's hold and faced me. "Excuse me, Mr. Tristan 'so goddamn superior he knows what's best for me' Stone. I came here long before I met you. Before you even fuckin' bought it. This was where I came to unwind. Do you have to ruin *everything* for me?"

"Stop being overdramatic, Maya."

Her dance partner stepped closer to us. "Hey buddy, is there a problem?"

"Stay out of it," I warned. "It's not your concern."

"No, I won't. We were having a good time until you came along." He got up into my face. "Who do you think you are anyway?"

"The owner of this club." I glared at him. "And you are dancing with my girl. Back off or I'll have you tossed out."

"Sorry, dude," he said, raising his hands in a conciliatory gesture. He nodded at Maya, and then walked toward the bar.

"I'm not your girl, Tristan!" Maya said. "You made that clear tonight when you fuckin' dumped me!"

"What are you going to do? Sleep with someone else?"

"Maybe. What do you care what I do? It's no longer your concern."

"Of course it is, Maya. Will you grow up and stop making a goddamn scene!"

"What are you going to do?" she said, her voice getting louder so people around us started to look. "Have one of the bouncers throw me out like you just threatened him?" She looked around the perimeter of the dance floor.

I leaned in close to her ear and seethed, "I'll throw you out on your sweet little ass myself if you continue to act like this." When I pulled back, our faces were inches apart. Her blue eyes burned with an intense fire and her breathing was ragged.

"Like what?"

"Like an immature—brat!"

"Fine. Maybe I am." She crossed her arms and raised her chin. "But at least I've been straight with you all along, not playing some game."

"What game? I've always cared for you. Only lately I started to have doubts about us."

Her lips quivered and she appeared to struggle to control her emotions. I could just pull her close now and kiss her. End this madness once and for all. Try to forget my irrational thoughts and my regretful words. Forget this horrid night ever happened.

Maya turned on her heel to storm through the crowd. I grabbed her hand at the last moment before she slipped away.

"I did it for you, Maya. Maybe one day you'll see that."

She squirmed out of my grasp. "Just leave me alone. You're nothing but a parasite. Use people and discard them when you no longer need them." She blinked away tears as if she was about to crumble and fought to hold a brave front. "Don't worry, I'll stay out of your precious club from now on."

My eyes followed her as she stormed out, until the final glow of her light disappeared out the main door.

A parasite who uses and discards people? What was she talking about? That wasn't me at all. Why didn't she get it?

And did I just make the biggest mistake of my life?

Too late now. What was done was done.

Fuck!

Maya

I took off my heels and walked down the road, fuming as the conversations from tonight replayed over and over in my mind.

Doubts? How could he doubt us? I may have doubts about a lot of things, but I believed in us.

A car pulled up beside me.

"Hey, babe, need a lift?"

"No!" I barked, not bothering to look. Of all the times I had to have some jerk accost me, jeez.

"It's me. From Vamps. We danced earlier tonight."

I looked up to see Nordic god from earlier.

"Oh, hey."

"What's wrong? You and your boyfriend have a fight?"

"Ex-boyfriend," I clarified. "And yes."

"Your feet must be killing you. Let me give you a lift. I promise I won't try anything."

Normally, I'd tell him thanks but no thanks. But there was nothing normal about tonight. I thought I'd be spending the night doing kinky things wrapped in the arms of my lover, not stumbling home barefoot and brokenhearted after being dumped without warning.

"Yeah, sure."

I climbed into his car. He pulled off and I gave him directions to my apartment.

"I'm Jed, by the way."

"Maya."

"Hey Maya, want to talk about what happened with that guy?"

"I'd rather not."

"Okay. If you don't mind me saying, that guy seems like a real jerk. You deserve to be treated better."

Tristan *had* treated me well. Until tonight. Well, we'd started to snip at each other over the past few days, but I didn't think anything of it.

Maybe I should have seen that it couldn't last. But I was too caught up in the affair that it was hard to look at it objectively.

Eventually, I'd get over it one day and move on.

But why wait?

I didn't want to go home alone tonight and cry over him. The hurt could wait until tomorrow.

When we reached my apartment, I turned to Jed. "Do you want to come in for a drink?"

CHAPTER 10

After a couple of glasses of wine on my couch and even a few laughs, Jed leaned forward and kissed me. For a moment, I froze.

This is what you need to forget about Tristan. Move on, sister!

I closed my eyes and kissed him back. Tristan's face appeared in my head.

Don't think of him. He dumped you, remember? You don't need those mind games.

I focused on Jed the best I could. *He kind of has an Eric from True Blood thing going on. Think of that.*

No use. Not even the fantasy of a hot Nordic vampire helped. All I could think of was Tristan. The way he kissed me. How he could light me on fire with both a tender touch and rough grasps. Tristan and his willingness to experiment with different ways to make sure sex was amazing. Tristan, who looked at me as if I was a goddess when I was on top of him. Tristan, who made sure I felt good—no, incredible.

Fuck! This wasn't working. Bad plan.

I pulled away from Jed. "I'm sorry, but I can't do this."

He squinted in confusion. "We can slow down if it's going too fast."

"No. I mean this." I motioned between us.

"O-kaaay," he said through gritted teeth. "You want me to go?"

I nodded. "Yeah. Sorry. It's too soon."

He stood and shrugged. "See you around."

After Jed left, I picked up a discarded shoe and threw it across the living room. It knocked over a cactus I loved and I instantly felt remorse. Seeing the dirt cascade over my rug reminded me when I knocked a plant over the first night I went to Tristan's. I was a clumsy fool. Clumsy in everything, especially relationships.

I salvaged the cactus, feeling guilty about my outburst. The cactus paid me back by pricking me several times. It was okay, I deserved it.

When Tristan called the next morning, I ignored it, still too angry at him to want to hear his voice—and now feeling guilty about kissing some guy the night before. In retrospect, that wasn't a good decision.

How do I get out of my own head?

I looked for my *Essential Nina Simone* album and put it on the record player. My grandmother gave it to me when she went into a nursing home and restoring it to good working condition was what I became fixated on after she died. It helped me stay connected to her. My grandparents always had a record playing and I inherited several albums that had survived over the years—anything from Elvis to classical to old comedy albums.

I pictured them playing records when they were younger, feeling love, happiness, sadness—all sorts of emotions to fit the mood. Maybe listening to comedy albums together. They were married for over fifty-five years. What was wrong with me then? A relationship I thought was the real thing didn't even last fifty-five days.

I put the record on and settled onto the sofa, staring at the ceiling as she sang about wanting sugar in her bowl. By the time she sang *Since I Fell for You*, the pull to call him back grew strong. But I couldn't. Not after what he'd done to me.

In the Dark didn't help matters. Memories of our sensual dances, hot nights in the lab, our time in his parents' garden, the cemetery…

Don't think about him! It's over.

When the album ended, I closed the record player cover and played music from my phone. I needed something else. After shuffling through my music collection, I stopped on Hole's *Live Through This* album. Perfect. Angrier. Raw. I sang along, close to screaming, like trying to rid myself of demons.

He doesn't care about how I feel. How could he if he broke my heart?

And when Courtney Love sang slower songs, I sang along, lamenting my loss.

How can I numb myself from this pain?

Hey, it was better this way. I didn't want to be in a relationship anyway, did I? I'd just thought he was hot. Now I could go on living my life.

What did people do to calm themselves in times of distress? Oh yes, they drank a cup of soothing tea. I could do that, despite my preference for coffee.

I boiled some water and did exactly what you're not supposed to do—I watched the kettle, waiting for the sound of a screaming banshee indicating that the water was ready. When it finally boiled several long minutes later, I grabbed a tea bag, tossed it into a mug, and poured hot water on it. Too bad I didn't have those fancy teacups like Tristan's parents had. A cute china teapot.

Stop! The tea is supposed to help you not *think of Tristan. You're not supposed to be reminded of the time you had tea with his family. Remember how his mother read your fortune?*

Fuck, fuck, fuck—get out of my head!

I gave up on my tea. Yet another reminder of him.

As the day went on, my anger dissipated. I remembered the times we spent together. Happy times. The sweet words we'd shared. How he called me beautiful or firecracker. How I thought we'd connected.

Why did he have to be such a jerk?

I found my Amy Winehouse playlist and put it on shuffle as I stared at the ceiling. When she sang *Back to Black*, I let myself wallow in the black despair of a broken heart. When *Our Day Will Come* came on, the pull returned.

I lit a candle and watched the flame. Fuck, would I ever look at a candle the same way again? *Damn you, Tristan Stone! I wish I'd never met you.*

Then I listened to *Love is a Losing Game*. And I listened to it twice more.

Don't think about him! It's over.

You Know I'm No Good played next. Guilt washed over me as I moved to the couch. Yeah, I probably shouldn't have gone with Jed.

But I didn't *cheat* on Tristan. He broke up with me. We were over.

I wished I had someone around to talk to about this. *Damn you, Nike. Where the hell are you?*

I sat down at my laptop to write her another e-mail she probably wouldn't read or respond to. But what else could I do with this excess energy and all these emotions that I didn't know what to do with? I couldn't just sit around and pine all day listening to music.

The email I wrote to Nike could probably be considered a short story. In it, I told her the whole shebang about how things had developed with Tristan. I even revealed my connection to fire, which I'd never told her about during the years we worked together at the firehouse. Being able to share with my best friend was something I'd wanted to do for ages. Whenever she'd called me her lucky charm when we went out on fire calls together, I had wanted to tell her why.

It felt good to get everything out of my confused head and written down. Finally, after feeling as if I'd been to confession, I fell asleep.

If I stayed in my apartment, I'd just sit around sulking while listening to music. So instead I worked whatever extra shifts I could at the firehouse. It was easy enough to get shifts since everyone else wanted to spend time with family with the holidays coming. I looked like hell. My movements were lethargic since I was just going through the motions, numb after all that exposure to raw pain.

Once again, my emotions were clearly displayed on my face to everyone who knew me. Why couldn't I master the art of the poker face?

Bob was the first one to approach me.

"You're sulking again," he said. "Boy troubles?"

"Isn't it always?" I snorted. I doodled on a notepad lying on a table in our lunch area.

"I'll give you the same advice I give my daughters. Find a way to distract yourself. Don't spend all your time thinking about some guy. It may or it may not work out. But your life goes on. So, live your life, Maya."

I stopped doodling and looked up at him. "That's actually pretty good advice. I'd do anything to get out of my own head right now."

"Then do something you enjoy. Or take on something new."

Later that day, Rick used his characteristic charm. "You look like ass, butt crunch. What's up with you lately?

"I don't want to talk about it." I tried to hold my lips in so I wasn't pouting.

"Fine, we won't talk about it," he said and leaned back in his chair. "But you need to do something to snap yourself out of it. Take a long bath, go to a spa, get a manicure or whatever girls do to make themselves feel good and look pretty. Maybe it will help get you out of your funk."

I crawled out of my hole of despair a bit to rise to his bait. "You know, you guys look like shit ninety percent of the time, so I don't want to hear it. You think you come in here all clean-shaven, smelling good and looking like a GQ model? Well, I hate to break it to you, but you don't. And just because I'm a woman doesn't mean I have to wear makeup and have my hair done every day and all that. If I feel like shit, maybe I don't care if I look like shit. And maybe you should cut me some friggin' slack and not give a damn either!"

Rick's eyes reflected his surprise before he recovered to clap a few times and smile. "Hot damn, it's about time we saw some of that fire back in you. You've been floating around here like a ghost. Maybe you'll be mad at me for stoking the flames, but I'm glad to see a flash of your old fiery self again."

Breathing hard after my outburst, I wasn't sure how to respond. Whatever he had wanted to do worked. Was I so easily manipulated?

I was also grateful that Rick was one of the few people I could unload my emotions on without him taking it personally.

I tried not to pout. "Shut up, butt crust."

Tristan called several times. Whenever he called, I'd stare at the ringing phone. Part of me wanted to pick up the phone and talk to him, ask him why he broke my heart, see if he'd come to his senses yet and beg me to come back to him. But if he didn't and was just explaining, I couldn't bear to listen to more reasons why we were wrong for each other. I couldn't take any more pain.

The other part of me wanted to pick up the phone, tell him to go fuck himself and hang up the phone on his stupid face.

When I wasn't working, I realized I needed to listen to Bob's advice and find a new hobby. Obviously, dancing at Vamps was not in my near future. Neither was checking out a live show there.

Maybe I should work out. Look for a gym. Try a new class. Nike used to go rock climbing. Maybe I should train to run a marathon or something. That might keep my mind focused for months as I worked through the pain of training.

Yeah, maybe not.

Who was I kidding? I was not joining a gym and I was most definitely never running a marathon.

I pulled on my favorite Type O Negative shirt over some comfy yoga pants and poured a glass of wine. As I tried to brainstorm ideas that would distract me from my breakup with Tristan, the doorbell rang.

I looked through the peephole. Was it Tristan begging for forgiveness?

No. But it was a welcome, joyous surprise.

"Nike!" I screamed and threw open the door.

CHAPTER 11

T*ristan*

Why wasn't she answering my calls?

This was getting ridiculous. Did it have to be like that? We couldn't even just talk about things?

Didn't she realize I did it for her own good? Because I cared about her?

Women. I didn't have much experience with them relationship-wise and it showed.

What should I do now? I thought of calling Mother to get her advice, but she was the one who got us into this mess to begin with. All that talk about light and darkness and working together. What did she know?

Or Dad. He'd lived with an eccentric woman for many years and he managed to stay sane.

Or maybe I could have Byron help smooth things over between Maya and me.

No, Byron worked for me. It would be unprofessional to ask him to help me with a personal problem.

Forget it. I tried to explain, but Maya wouldn't listen.

Fine, let her go on with her life and I'd go on with mine. It would be as if we never knew each other.

But we did.

Everywhere I looked carried a memory of her. The lab. Vamps. My loft. I remembered her laughter, the passion we shared, how she chased the darkness away and brought me a comfort I'd never known.

On an exhale, I closed my eyes. Letting her into my life had been stupid. It made it all the harder to forget her.

I had to get out of the lab. Go walk along the ocean and clear my head. The salty scent and rolling waves was always a balm to the chaos of life.

Once I strode along a path near the shore, I inhaled in search of the soothing effect.

Maya and I had strolled there.

Further ahead was the cemetery. Oh shit, that was where it had all begun. The things I'd revealed to her. The sensuality…

Oh God. How could I get her out of my head? Was there a potion I could brew to make me forget her?

I picked up the phone. "Dad, do you have a minute?" I then gave him a condensed version, removing all the sexy parts a parent did not want to hear. I sighed. "I don't know what I'm supposed to do."

"First off, you need to figure out what you want, Tristan. You sound confused. Do you want to be with her? Or do you want her to forgive you to alleviate your guilt and find some closure?"

"I don't know."

"Two very different options. Once you know what you want, you just have to put yourself out there. What happens might fit in with what you want, or you could get burned. But life and love are full of risks. And you know what they say about the bigger one is, the bigger the other is as well. But at least you know you've tried your best."

I paced as we spoke. "Even if I want to be with her and for some unlikely reason she still wants to be with me, how do we make it work? She's so—impulsive. And I'm so—well, you know what I'm like. Why would someone so passionate and beautiful and crazy as she is, want to be with someone like me? She could have anyone."

"Maya is right about one thing. She is a grown woman and capable of making her own decisions. We may not understand why women love us fools, but they do."

Maybe so. "But how do people so different make it work? Like you and Mother. Your personalities aren't alike at all. But yet, you've been married for years."

"Relationships are tough, Tristan. Your mother and I faced bumps like everyone does as we figured out how we could live together. The only thing I can say is let her be her and you need to be you."

I thought about that for a minute. Dad was a man of few words and often spoke in abstracts rather than giving detailed responses. But I thought I got the gist.

Now what to do about my predicament?

Maya

I gave Nike the biggest hug I could and said, "Come in, come in."

"Maya, it's so good to see you. I'm so sorry it's been so long."

"Since the fire," I said.

"I know," she said. "That was a crazy night. The start of some massive life changes."

"You look—different," I said. "What is it?" I looked her up and down to try to place it. "You still look like you, still have that hot dark-red hair and kickass body, but something is—not like you."

Nike took a deep breath. "I know."

When she didn't elaborate, I prompted her, "Well?"

"There's a reason I haven't been back. It's not because I haven't wanted to. It's because I didn't think I should."

"Why not?"

"Things happened after the fire. Things that may have changed me forever."

"Was it Michel?" I said, puffing up. "What did he do to you? I'll kill the bastard! Fuckin' men! We're so much better without those assholes!"

"It's not Michel," Nike said, placing her hands on my shoulders to subdue me. "He's been nothing but wonderful to me, taking care of me."

"Then what is it? Are you sick? Tell me, Nike. My brain is already racing, thinking the worst."

"It's related to Michel. Or what he is." She took my hand and said, "You may want to sit down for this."

Nike paced before me. "So, the night of the fire, well, I know what happened."

I squirmed in my seat. "We knew it was arson, but they haven't yet found out who was responsible."

"It was Ricard. He'd been hunting Michel down for years, ever since they were turned."

"Who's that? And turned? Into what?"

"You have to swear to keep this between us."

What the heck was she about to tell me? Who was this Ricard dude and what was with the turning?

"Ricard and Michel were attacked centuries ago. Bitten by a woman and turned into—you're going to think I'm nuts and I would too if I were you. But considering you revealed what you can do with fire, I'm hoping you can be more open to a bigger world out there. Bigger than I'd ever imagined."

Thinking of Tristan's way of seeing people and his mother's ability to communicate with the dead, I said, "I'm learning all kinds of things about people lately. So, don't worry about me being narrow-minded."

"They were attacked and turned into nightwalkers. That's what Michel calls them, but they're essentially vampires."

Nike stopped talking and stared, as if waiting for my reaction. The questioning look on her face led me to believe she expected me to laugh or call her insane.

"Seriously?"

"Seriously."

"Fuck me," was all I could say.

She laughed somewhat with relief. "Want me to go on?"

I made an exaggerated gesture as if bracing myself and then said, "Go on. I have to hear the rest of this story."

She continued by telling me how she and Michel were hunted and how Ricard and another vampire attacked her.

"Michel destroyed them. For good. Their ashes were washed out to sea." She bit her lip and added, "Since Ricard bit me, I haven't been the same. I don't really know what's going on with me. Neither does Michel. I'm not like him, but I'm not like how I was either."

"What do you mean?"

"I'm different. My senses have been affected. Sight, smell, hearing, all much improved. I feel things differently than I used to. I react much quicker to things—in different ways. Not only are my reflexes quicker, but I fly off the handle at little provocation. I have to control my temper from getting the best of me."

What the fuck happened to my best friend? "What have you been doing all this time?"

"We've been trying to understand what exactly is happening to me. So far, we haven't found anyone with the answers. I've been trying to adjust, basically. Michel has been helping me, watching me to see if I become like him, and if I do, he'll help me over. But we both know it would be too difficult to go back to my old life right now. I can't work at the firehouse. I mean, look at me. It's obvious something is up."

"It's been awhile since people have seen you and it's not as obvious as you might think. They might not notice. I mean I didn't look at you and think, 'Holy shit! She's turned into some sort of vampire!'"

Nike burst out laughing. "I almost forgot how you could make me laugh. But seriously, thanks for saying that. I don't know what I'm going to do just yet." She stopped pacing and sat next to me.

"Why didn't you come to me?" I asked, trying to keep the hurt out of my voice and pretty sure I failed.

"I called you after the fire. But I didn't think I could see you in person. How would you react? I didn't know how to explain it. I still don't. Michel warned me that if I was changing, I'd be a danger to you and others. And it was too difficult to stay away. So we left. If I was physically an ocean away from everyone, it would be easier to avoid them. I couldn't bear to hurt the people I cared about."

"Do you feel an urge to hurt me?"

"No, I don't. Thank God. But I'm not the way I was. I can feel the difference."

"Are you a vampire?"

"No. I don't think so." She shrugged. "We think Ricard's bite acted more like an infection rather than a transformation. Whether the effect will exacerbate or fade, we don't know."

"What about drinking blood?"

She stared at me as if gauging what to tell me. "I haven't *attacked* a human to drink blood."

"What are you not telling me?"

"Well, I've tried blood. And I liked it."

I tried to keep the horror off my face. "Human?"

She turned her head and ignored the question. Why? Did she think I'd freak out?

"Can you go out in the sun?"

"Yes. It hurts my eyes, but I just wear a hat and sunglasses. But, it's hardly ever happened because I sleep during the day, wake up at night. Courtesy of living with Michel."

"Do you guys sleep in—coffins?"

"No. We sleep in beds. Michel knows the ins and outs of which hotels to go to."

"Of course he does," I said, trying to bite back the sarcasm.

Nike caught it. "He's been good to me."

I planted my hands on my hips. "Technically, he's the reason your life has changed. Why you've had to stay away from everyone."

"I made my choices that night, Maya. And he's the reason I didn't end up dead on a beach."

Changing the subject before I said something negative, I said, "So, now you're back?"

"When I read your e-mails, I could sense what you weren't telling me. You were confused and in pain. You're obviously going through something with this guy Tristan. Something big enough that you reached out to me. And no matter what, you're still my closest friend. I had to come see you. And your revelation about the fire thing—how could I not respond to that? Remember how I always said you were my lucky charm?"

I nodded.

"Whenever I went out on a call, I hoped you'd be with me. Anyway, we felt safe enough that I wouldn't be any danger to you. And since you'd been hiding your own little secret for years, I figured you probably wouldn't freak out too much when you heard mine." Nike paused. "So, I finally told you about what's happened with me. What about you? You gave me a quick update in your email."

"Okay. Your timing couldn't be better. I really need a friend right now. I'm so confused," I said. "But I think I need to open a bottle of Beaujolais Nouveau before I start. You can still drink wine, can't you?"

Nike smiled like the Cheshire cat. "It tastes better now than ever."

We hung out for hours, killing a bottle of wine as we caught up on the last several months, leading up to my wild affair with Tristan. The best part now was this new openness we had between us. I'd never told her about my gift with fire and now with her condition, well—there were only so many people you could confide your deepest darkest secrets to.

And now with our guy issues. It had been ages since either of us were in a relationship, which was why the two of us had spent many of our Saturday nights off together at Vamps. Now we weren't just smitten, but smitten with guys with their own little supernatural quirks. Well, my affair was over and now I was mostly brokenhearted and confused.

"Why would he do that to me, Nike? We were so good together. We had the best time. Someone who you could work with and spend your free time with and not want to kill is rare."

"Like us," she said.

"In a way, yes," I said. "He has that reserved side to him, like you have."

"Maybe we both go for the opposites attract thing," Nike suggested. "You and I are like night and day. And Michel has that *let's go experience everything the world has to offer* part of his personality."

"Perhaps," I agreed. "But my relationship with Tristan fell apart while our friendship is still strong, despite how long it's been since I've seen you." Shaking my head, I added, "I don't know. One thing different is that Tristan and I screwed every chance we could."

"Yup, a bit different." She laughed, but then turned serious. "Have you spoken to him since?"

"No." I crossed my arms. On realizing the classic defensive posture, I forced myself to drop my arms to my side.

"Why not?"

"I don't answer the phone when he calls. Why should I? *He* broke up with *me*. I don't want to hear his excuses so he can make *himself* feel better. I'm *not* going to tell him it's okay. It's not friggin' okay. Look at me. I'm a hideous mess. See these bags under my eyes? I haven't had a good night sleep since I don't know when. And I love my sleep!"

"Oh, Maya. My temperamental friend. Just talk to the guy, will ya? When your temper goes down, have a normal conversation."

My gaze settled on the rug. "I'm afraid of how much it would hurt. Or, how I might be tempted to kill him."

She squeezed my upper arm and smiled. "Just make sure you don't bring any sharp objects, so as not to tempt yourself."

"But—"

"Uh-oh. But what?"

"There's a new little issue that complicates things."

"What?" she asked warily.

"I kissed someone else."

"Oh my. Who?"

"Just some guy. I don't know why!" I protested, "I was super vulnerable at the moment. Tristan had just dumped me and I felt like shit. This guy I'd danced with offered me a ride home. I wanted to distract myself from all the negative shit going round and round in my head, but it didn't help. It only made me compare him to Tristan and miss him even more."

Nike took a deep breath and exhaled. "Well, it's only a kiss. Not like it's the end of the world."

"Nope," I agreed.

"And it's not like a million people haven't done the same thing in your shoes. Or much more."

"Yup." I nodded.

"You can't undo it. So just move on."

I bit my lip. "Now what? Do I tell Tristan? I mean, if I ever talk to him again? It meant nothing. I mean, people kiss each other on the lips all the time in greeting and all."

"Hmm," Nike said. "Would you want him to tell you?"

I leaned back. The image of Tristan kissing someone else made me squeeze my eyes shut, trying to force it away. "Yes." I reopened my eyes. "I wouldn't like it, but I wouldn't want him keeping things from me."

Nike spread her palms up. "Then there you go."

"I'm screwed." I dropped my head into my hands. "And I'm so mad at him still. I don't know what to do. I don't even know how I feel. Fuck, I'm such an idiot."

Nike smiled. "But such an endearing one."

Tristan

Distracting myself wasn't working. I couldn't forget her. If she wouldn't take my calls, I'd go to her place. I walked to her apartment, arguing with myself the entire way.

What are you doing, fool? She doesn't want to see you.

We need to talk. It can't end the way it did.

I reached her front door and rang the bell.

"You forget something?" Maya asked as she opened the door, but then her mouth dropped. Her face contorted into all sorts of emotions—surprise, joy, anguish, rage—I couldn't keep up.

"You were expecting someone else?"

"What are you doing here?" she spat.

"Can I come in?"

"For what?"

"To talk."

"If you're here to explain how we're so wrong for each other, how it was a mistake, I don't want to hear it again. I get it. It's over. We're done."

"Please. Just let me in."

Her breathing was rapid as she swung the door open to let me enter. She then slammed it shut. As she stood there with arms crossed, the soft light around her now pinged with a flaming red border. I was so mesmerized by seeing color around a person for the first time that I almost forgot why I was here.

"Who did you think I was?"

"Nike, not that it's any of your business. She just left."

"Your friend who you told me about?"

She ignored my question. Through clenched teeth, she said, "Go on. Speak."

"Please don't talk to me like that. I thought you deserved better than me. Someone without all my baggage to contend with. I would do anything to be normal, to be able to go out with you in public and not feel horrified by shadows slinking around people. So, I can't be the companion you deserve. As much as I want to be that person, I'm not. I did what I thought was best—for you."

"What *you* thought was best for *me*?" She pointed at my chest and then hers. "Who gave *you* the power to decide what's best for me? I'm an adult. I've been in my skin a long time. If I didn't want to be with someone, if I didn't think I could handle their quirks, I wouldn't be with them."

"Maya, I—"

"No, I'm not done. Has it ever occurred to you that maybe I enjoyed trying to help you? That maybe not only was I attracted to you, but that I liked to feel needed? That I'm not just a firefighter because I'm a freak with a connection to fire, but that I actually want to help people? How dare you presume to know me and what's best for me!"

She crossed her arms and pouted.

"I asked you not to speak to me like that! You're right. We are adults. Stop shouting and sulking like a child and speak to me like an adult!" I realized I was now the one shouting and how tense my body was. Shit, I had to calm down. Why was she getting under my skin like that? I had to regain control.

"You know what, Tristan." She waved one arm. "If you don't want the crazy, don't push the crazy buttons." She raised both arms to the heavens. "I hate it when people try to make decisions for me. Try to control me. I moved here myself, built a career, have a decent apartment—I think I can pretty much fuckin' take care of myself."

"I am not trying to control you, Maya." I unclenched my fists and held one hand out to her in a conciliatory gesture.

She shook her head. "Forget it. I have nothing more to say to you, Tristan Stone. We had some fun together. That's all it was— fun. And that time is obviously over. I don't want to have some discussion to end this with *closure*. And I don't want to *still be friends*."

"Are you kidding me? Dismissing me like I'm some guy you picked up in a club for the night?" Her eyes darted off. "Don't play with me like that, Maya."

"That *is* all it was, wasn't it? We fooled around. We did stupid shit pretending to do spells and all that crap. What were we thinking?"

"Goddammit, Maya. Do you know how infuriating you are?" I marched over to her and looked into her eyes, which were now blazing with anger. "Don't put up this mask, steeling yourself against me. I know what you're doing. You can't fool me with this brave front. I know you better than you think."

Her blue eyes burned with tears of both rage and sadness. "Then do you know how badly you hurt me? I let you in; I shared my secrets with you. And you just threw it all away because things didn't go the way you'd planned. If anyone is acting like an immature, spoiled brat, it's you!"

She moved to walk away, but I grabbed her by the shoulders. "Look at me."

"No." She squared her shoulders. "Leave me alone."

"I said, look at me, Maya!" My tone startled her enough that she finally relented. "You don't think I feel this too? That I'm heartless? A robot?"

She looked away again, trying to struggle out of my grasp. "You're just some guy. No different from the rest. I should've stayed away from you that night I first met you. I never believe the shit guys say. I mean, come on, I've heard it all. I should know better. But something about you made me think you were different. I was wrong. So fuckin' wrong. I'm such an idiot! Let go of me."

"No. I'm not going to let you run away and avoid me. Let's deal with this now."

She seethed, but stopped struggling to escape my grasp. "Fine."

"You weren't wrong. The things I said—they were all sincere, not some lines. My feelings for you were real. No, they *are* real."

Her eyes were filled with such pain, I just wanted to pull her close and make it go away. What killed me was that I was the source of the pain. By caring for her and trying to protect her, I had caused her all this anguish. For someone without much experience with relationships, I was finding out the hard way how difficult and complicated they could be.

"I was good for you, I know it," Maya replied, blinking back tears. "And you were good for me. Then why did you have to be such a dumbass and throw away something so fuckin' great?"

"I don't know!" I raised my arms and paced. "Don't you think I ask myself that question every day?"

"No. How would I know that?"

"I haven't stopped thinking about you."

"Don't feed me lines, Tristan. I'm not a game to be played, I'm a human being."

I stopped before her. "Not lines, Maya. No games. I want you back in my life. Dammit all to hell if I'm being selfish. But. I. Want. You."

CHAPTER 12

The struggle she felt on hearing those words was clearly shown through the expressions playing out on her face. From what I interpreted, she wanted to believe me and come back to me. But she also had to be tough and protect herself.

She turned her head. "No. I may have been a fool once, but I'm not going to be fooled again. I'm a big girl and that means taking care of myself. So, I have to protect myself from situations—and people—who hurt me. And *you* hurt me."

"Look me in the eye, Maya. I would do anything to avoid hurting you again. I would inflict countless wounds on myself before I ever let any harm come to you."

Her eyes flitted all over the room, avoiding mine.

"Maya, you know me better than anyone else." I placed my hand over my heart. "Hurting you kills me, tears my very soul apart."

Her brave front was weakening, her lips quivering. Her eyes still darted as she tried to regain control of her warring emotions.

"Look at me."

"I can't."

"Why not?"

"A part of me wants to believe you and try to start fresh. But, I did something stupid. And I'm afraid to tell you."

"Tell me." I clenched my fist. What the hell was coming?

"Are you sure you want to hear it?"

I nodded without looking at her.

"Honesty over hurting your feelings?"

I gritted my teeth. "Yes."

"Even if it's brutal honesty?"

"Damn it, Maya. Just tell me. The more you delay it, the worse things I think."

"Okay." She took a deep breath and spoke quickly. "I kissed someone else."

"You what?" The horrible speculation that my imagination had concocted had merit.

"It was nothing. Just a kiss. I was trying to forget you. It didn't work."

"With—who?"

"That guy you saw me dancing with the other night."

"You—and that—that—meathead?"

She shrugged. "Yeah. And it sucked, by the way."

I grabbed my temples and resumed pacing. "I don't want to hear the details."

"I'm sorry. I wasn't thinking right. And I just wanted to get you out of my head."

"You." My eyes bulged out of my skull. "And him?" Words were failing me.

"But it didn't work. I kept thinking about you and how much I missed you and how you broke my heart. And how much I wished he was you."

"You cheated on me?"

She shook her head. "How could I cheat on you if we weren't together? You freakin' ended it, remember? We weren't *on a break.* We were fuckin' broken. You severed it."

The vision of her and someone else stung so much I could barely listen to anything else. "You *kissed* that guy?"

"Tristan, you're not listening to me! I'm telling you how it was a mistake. I was trying to forget you. You hurt me and I lashed out. I wanted to hurt you too, I guess. I don't know what I was thinking—so many crazy things. I didn't feel anything for him. I just didn't want to feel any more for you."

"I bet *he* felt *a lot* of you."

She recoiled when I said that and I instantly regretted it.

In a soft voice, she said, "I'm sorry."

My chest constricted and I found it difficult to breathe. "I have to get out of here."

I stormed out her front door.

"Tristan, wait."

I raised my hand up to stop her, without looking back. "No more, Maya. No."

How could she do that to me? With him? Only hours—not days or weeks—after we'd broken up and she went off with someone else?

I prowled the shore, seeking answers, barely aware of the biting cold coming off the Atlantic tonight, but tightening my trench coat anyway.

His lips kissed hers, his hands touched her body… She was mine!

If I saw him right now, I would rip him apart. He'd probably return to the club one day. I'd watch for him, waiting. I'd told him she was my girl that night and yet he still went after her.

He took what was mine. He had to pay.

I COULDN'T GET the images of them together out of my mind. Sure, Maya had lovers before me, but seeing one of them, talking to him, knowing that he kissed and touched my girl tormented me.

My cell phone rang. It was Maya.

I couldn't hear her voice right now. Just earlier the same voice confessed an act that ripped through my soul.

When I listened to her voicemail, it said, "Tristan. I'm filled with regret about what happened. I'm so sorry."

I hurled the phone into the Atlantic and kept on walking. When I passed the cemetery, I refused to look inside, refused to feel any sort of longing for her.

She betrayed me.

How could she do this to me?

I should go back to Vamps right now and pick someone up, bring her back to my loft, and violate her in fifty ways. Let's see how Maya would feel about that.

She would feel hurt. Like I am now.

She'd know this pain burning through me.

But wait—she was already hurt before she did this. It's why she did it.

I hurt her.

No! I loved her and she broke my heart! How can I ever forgive her for what she's done to me?

And yet, I expect her to forgive me for what I've done to her.

Fuck. Did I just think—I love her?

Do I love her? Is this what love feels like? From unimaginable ecstasy to unfathomable pain?

Why did I have to fuckin' break both of our hearts to figure it out?

I meandered without destination for hours, replaying what she had said earlier that night as I had been too disturbed to take it in. My soul felt like it was tearing itself apart. It had to be darker than any of the ones I'd ever encountered.

In honesty, how could I blame the guy for wanting to be with her? Who could resist Maya's charms? Her beauty?

She was right. She hadn't cheated on me. I had ended it. I had let her go, which meant she was free to be with whomever she wanted.

Maya was right. I was a dumbass. And I threw away the best thing that ever happened to me.

I have no one to blame but myself. All this pain, this torment—I did this to both of us.

My mind was still restless, but my feet were weary so I headed back to my loft. I didn't know what to do at this point. How could I fix something that I'd fucked up so utterly?

There, sitting on the stairwell in front of the entrance, was my light, my angel, wiping away tears. And then there were no more questions. The solution—the key—was right before me.

"Maya? What are you doing here?"

"Tristan." She stood up. Her brilliant blue eyes were filled with so much pain and regret, a look I never wanted to see in them again. "Losing you hurt so much. I didn't want to feel it anymore."

"Shhh. I know. Don't talk right now."

I opened my arms and she rushed into them. I pressed my lips on hers. The taste of her soft lips reignited my passion for her I'd been trying to subdue, only now it roared with a renewed intensity after being denied for so long. I ran my fingers through her hair, inhaling her heavenly scent.

"I missed you so much, Maya. It was unbearable. How could I have been so stupid to let you go?" I slid my hands down her body, wanting to touch every inch of her.

"I missed you too. So much."

Take her upstairs. Throw her on the bed. Show her how much you fuckin' love her.

No. Slow it down. Take it easy.

Reluctantly, I pulled away from her lips and wiped away what remained of her tears.

"As much as I want you right now, we should slow it down. We've hurt each other. Everything ignited so quickly with us, it was bound to burn up in flames. I want to take it slow. Do it right. Are you okay with that?

Her eyes hooded, she looked up at me. "Yes."

"Good. I'm sorry I hurt you, Maya. If I learned anything from it, it's that I don't want to let you go. I never want to hurt you again."

"I'm sorry I hurt you, too."

"I'm going to call you a taxi, before I take you upstairs and do what my body is aching to do. But will you meet me tomorrow night?"

"I don't know," she said. "Maybe. I don't even know why I came here tonight."

"Yes, you do."

Her beautiful eyes fixed on mine. "You're right. I do. I had to see you."

"I'm going to try to be a better match for you, Maya. I don't want to keep you from the world. And with you at my side, it's easier to interact with people in it."

She placed her hand over her heart. "Oh, Tristan."

"How about we start again slowly? I'll meet you at Vamps tomorrow night for a drink. Maybe a dance."

She looked away as if trying to stifle a smile threatening to cross her face. "Perhaps."

"We can even go on a double date with another couple, if you'd like. Slow things down and be more like a normal couple, go out to dinner or the movies, rather than experiment with potions and in graveyards."

When she looked back at me, she had a twinkle in her eye. "Normal is overrated. But I'd like that."

It took all my willpower not to kiss her senseless and bring her to my loft. Instead, I kissed her hand, and said, "Get some sleep, my beautiful girl. Until tomorrow."

CHAPTER 13

M *aya*

     The emotional roller coaster I'd been stuck on left me unsure if I was coming or going these days. Had I ever gone through a whirlwind of such that I'd experienced lately? From exhilaration to despair and back to cautious optimism. I didn't even think the wild mood swings when I was an angst-ridden teenager compared, when I struggled to figure out why I was so different from everyone else.

If I was wearing a mood ring right now, it would blare with whatever color symbolized excitement—breath-stealing anticipation as I looked forward to meeting Tristan tonight. After finally having a good night sleep, the day started out brighter than it had been since our break up.

I put on a sexy, tight, black number. Funny how many of these dresses I had in my closet. This one was long-sleeved and fitted from the tops of the shoulders down to around the knees, where it flared out down to my ankles. Feminine yet sexy. It showed off my curves in a flattering manner.

After taking a cab to the waterfront area, I strolled down the alley between the warehouses, smiling to myself as I thought about the promising night ahead. Why did I ever think this alley was creepy? It led directly to my happiness.

We were starting up again. Starting it right, going slow.

In my anticipation of seeing Tristan again, I was early for once. Super early. But maybe having a drink and dancing would help me relax a little bit. Decompress to get rid of some of the negative energy I'd had festering inside me when I thought we were over.

After chatting with Byron for a few, I went to the bar. Maddie and Roderick, the couple I'd met before my breakup with Tristan, were sitting at the bar watching the crowd.

"Hi!" I said, unable to contain my excitement at meeting Tristan.

"Maya, what a pleasant surprise," Maddie said. "How have you been?"

"Oh. You know. Things are crazy as usual," I said with a wave of my hand. "You?"

"Fine, thanks." She looked at me for a second or two before continuing. "We were hoping to hear from you."

"Sorry. Like I said, things have been pretty hectic. But I think they will be getting back to normal."

"Glad to hear it," Roderick said. "Can we get you a drink?"

"Sure. I'd love a Tempting Fate."

After Roderick handed me my drink, Maddie asked, "Are you meeting your boyfriend?"

I nodded while I sipped the decadent drink through the straw, so quickly I almost had brain freeze. "Yes. But I'm really early. He probably won't be here for a while."

"Hang with us," Roderick said.

"We don't bite," Maddie added. "Unless you want us to."

Once again, my body was giving me mixed signals in response to her obvious advances. Not knowing what to say, I smiled.

"You and your guy are such an attractive couple," she said. "We'd love to have you at one of our parties," Maddie said.

"Um, maybe. One day."

"Maybe you should come and check out our place, where we host parties. You know, see if you and your boyfriend want to come by one day."

"Yeah, well, I'm meeting him here later so tonight's probably not good."

"What time?"

"An hour and a half."

"Oh, don't worry," Maddie replied with a carefree wave. "We have plenty of time. We live close by. We can walk there. Let's go check it out. And we'll come right back here. Just think of the little surprise you could give your boyfriend. What guy wouldn't get excited about a suggestion like that?"

Roderick rubbed Maddie's shoulders and then nuzzled her neck. "Every guy I know would be thrilled if his girlfriend was open to—options."

Options, eh? Hmm. Tristan was trying to interact more in the world for my sake. He'd even suggested a double date with another couple. This might not be what he had in mind, but hey, it might be easier for him, if not enjoyable. After all, sex was quite a delicious distraction. I could present him with a sexy little surprise…

Wait, we said we'd take things slow. Suggesting a couples' party didn't seem all that slow.

Hmm, he was into sexual experimentation and this would be a kinky surprise. Spice things up, perhaps. I didn't know how Tristan would react about partying with another couple —or multiple couples—but why not find out more and offer up the option?

Stop overanalyzing. Get out of your damn head. Don't think about every possibility and just find out already.

"Yeah, okay." I shrugged. "Why not?"

On the way out, I left word with Byron. "If Tristan is looking for me, tell him I'll be right back."

Byron gave the couple I was leaving with a quick once-over. "Okay, see ya soon, Maya."

Tristan

When I came upstairs, I was surprised to see Maya there already. She was talking to a couple at the bar. They had dark shadows surrounding them, which repelled me. Still, I had to approach them and be social for Maya's sake. If we were going to be together, I couldn't be some creepy guy who brooded from the shadows.

I focused on Maya's light to help. But by the time I'd braced myself to walk over to say hello, they walked toward the exit.

Where was she going? And who were these people?

My imagination started to get the best of the situation.

She changed her mind. You hurt her too much. She made new friends and is going someplace with them.

Jilting you.

She's just playing with you, you fool. She probably just agreed to come here tonight so you'd stop bugging her.

Shit, I ruined everything, didn't I?

Not really knowing what I was doing, I walked down the stairwell to go back to my lab. But instead, I exited through a door downstairs. I followed around to the front of the building, staying close to the shadows. I could hear the women's heels on the pavement before I could see them. They were chatting about something, but I couldn't make it out. The guy walked quietly with them.

I scanned the couple. A curvy, dark-haired woman and a slim man with a pointy Van Dyke.

Did Maya know them? Or had she just met them?

I followed them through the alley, staying far enough

back to avoid being spotted. But, I couldn't make out what they were saying.

One part of me was hell-bent on finding out what Maya was doing. If she had decided not to try again, she could have at least let me know.

But then why was she at Vamps to begin with? We weren't supposed to meet for another hour or two. Why would she come early and then leave?

Another part of me was disgusted with myself.

You do realize that what you're doing is stalking her? Like an obsessed boyfriend. Or ex-boyfriend. Or whatever the hell you are to her right now. Why don't you leave her alone? If she wants to get on with her own life—a life without you—you ought to let her do it.

If that's the case, why wouldn't she just let me know? I can't let her leave, walk out of my life, without knowing.

They strolled away from the warehouse district and the water to a residential neighborhood. They turned onto a street that appeared to be a cul-de-sac. It was harder to cloak myself as we moved into this area. I tried to stick behind trees large enough to conceal my presence with their dark, sweeping shadows. And hoping no neighbors peered out their windows to see some suspicious man creeping behind trees on their street.

The three of them walked into a white colonial with black shutters at the far end of the cul-de-sac.

Okay. Now what? What am I going to do now? Just sit out here and wait?

Wait for what?

I couldn't really sit out on this quiet little road all night without arousing some suspicion. So, I stuck to the main road. Walking up and down it wouldn't strike anyone as odd as much as if I paced around the cul-de-sac. Plus, if Maya came out, I should be able to see her when she returned to the main road.

If she came back out tonight.

You know, Tristan, you are really going too far. This is some serious, twisted shit. Following her? You should just go back to the club. If Maya wants to see you, she knows where to find you.

I ignored the voice nagging me and paced the road, trying to look like a pleasant chap out for a little stroll this evening.

Maya

Although the exterior of this house on this peaceful cul-de-sac looked welcoming, the second I stepped inside, I had second thoughts. Did I really just go home with a couple of strangers? Am I not a firefighter who should have a little more common sense than this? What the hell was wrong with me lately—I definitely wasn't thinking straight.

Oh yes—lust. Or, I don't know—more than that. A relationship with Tristan. Maybe even love?

No, I couldn't think like that. He already broke my heart and I hurt him. I couldn't think of the big L word.

"Make yourself at home, Maya," Maddie said with a welcoming wave.

I sat down on an oversized taupe sofa. The living room colors were neutral, probably eggshell or some other poor excuse of a wall color that I hated. What was so wrong with putting some color into your world? It's a living room, so live in it.

Maddie sat across from me and crossed her tanned legs. She appraised me from head to toe.

More questions swarmed around in my head. Would I be expected to fool around with Maddie? Or Roderick? Or both? Did I want to? Or maybe we'd just be fooling around with our partners with the excitement of being watched. That might be okay. I didn't know if I was ready to share Tristan yet. And he probably wasn't ready to share me. But, how would I know how he'd react?

"I'll get us all some drinks," Roderick said.

"So, how long have you and your boyfriend been together?" Maddie asked. "What's his name?"

"Tristan," I said. "Not too long. It got pretty intense pretty quickly."

She smiled. "Maybe you realized you were right for each other."

Hmm. I did think that at one point. But then again, I didn't think he'd dump me the way he had. Or that I'd hurt him. "I don't know. Maybe."

Roderick returned with some drinks in martini glasses. "For two beautiful women," he said as he handed a glass to each of us. "How about a toast?"

"To the start of a new friendship," Maddie said.

Friends with benefits was what they meant, I'd bet. "Cheers."

We clinked glasses and took a sip. Ugh, whatever was in the glass was hard liquor and it tasted like ass. Okay, maybe not to people who drank it, but I'd grown used to the girly drinks at Vamps, which were sweet and fruity. Hard liquor was definitely not my thing.

"Something wrong?" Maddie asked.

Forcing the horrid expression off my face so as not to appear rude, I said, "I'm fine. But could you excuse me for a moment to use your bathroom?"

"Of course," Maddie said. "Right down the hall. First door on the right."

Once in the bathroom, I emptied the drink down the sink and refilled it with water. They'd never know. And I wouldn't have to force down that awful crap.

I checked my appearance and refreshed my lipstick. Then I returned to the living room. We sat down and chit-chatted for a while. We talked about Vamps, the music and so on. How it was the only club in the area that they really liked. We told each other about our day jobs. They were both in sales and marketing, but for different companies. They told me how long they'd been married and lived in the area. I evaded as many questions as I could about how long Tristan and I had been together, because truthfully it was just a speck compared to their eight years together. And then we got into the nitty-gritty of what really went on.

"Basically, Maya, we're just a normal couple with day jobs who enjoy the company of other couples," Maddie said. "Sometimes we'll just have another couple over. Sometimes we'll have four or five at a party."

"And what *really* happens at these parties?" I forced the image of a wild gangbang out of my head.

"Well, we might have a couple of drinks, like we're doing now," Roderick said.

"And then we'll go into another room. If anyone wants to play, we play," Maddie finished.

I was pretty sure they meant sexually, but didn't want to come right out and ask. I mean, how would I know what went on at parties like this? I'd certainly never been to one. I didn't know if I'd like it, but I had to admit, I was a little curious.

"Could you show me the room?" I asked.

"Of course," Maddie said. "Come this way."

"Looks as if you finished your drink," Roderick said. "Let's get you a refill."

"No. I'm good, thanks."

"You sure?" He squinted as he looked at me.

"Yes, I'm fine."

I followed Maddie down the hall and checked her out from behind. She was definitely attractive with her straight dark hair and shapely figure. If I was going to bat for the other team as they'd say, she'd definitely be a contender.

Roderick, well, I didn't know about him. His facial hair

accentuated his pointy face. He was attractive but in an off-putting way—one of those guys with a scary form of attractiveness. Was it his quiet nature? No, Tristan was also quite reserved, yet it was one of the things that drew me to him. His mysterious, brooding nature intrigued me, and led me to want to take care of him.

But Roderick and his black eyes. So different from Tristan's dark ones. The way Roderick looked at me didn't sit right. The first time I met them, I felt it subconsciously and chose to focus on Maddie instead. She was far more exuberant. In fact, I still focused more on her. Roderick, though, I didn't know what made his look so unsettling. Was it coldness in his eyes? Or was it lust? If the latter, I didn't think I wanted to be any part of his shenanigans.

Maddie opened the door to a large room. Although it appeared to be a regular sitting room at first, it was without a doubt an adult playroom. There were a couple of mismatched couches, several cushions, and bean bag chairs strewn about. In the corner on the left was a dark oak bar with several types of glasses on top. A few small tables around the room had baskets with condoms in them as well as vibrators and other sex toys. In a far corner was a swing. I was pretty sure it was not your average playground type. A fireplace graced the middle of the long wall. Opposite the fireplace was a padded table of some sort, like the kind a masseuse would have. Only this version had restraints on each corner. Windows on two of the walls had dark curtains pulled shut, for obvious reasons.

Hmm. Maybe this was something that I'd find alluring one day. But seeing it here and now killed my curiosity. In a few years time, if Tristan and I were still together, we could consider exploring new sexual options.

We better still be together, a voice inside me scolded.

Whatever fantasies I might have entertained on the way

over here were squashed by the reality of the room and all it had to promise. I was not interested in this kind of lifestyle.

All I wanted was Tristan. I wanted to be with him and only him. More than anything, I wanted to be back at Vamps with him right now.

Why did I come here?

"As you can see," Maddie said, "there are different things for different tastes."

"I see."

"Do you see anything you like?"

"Umm—it's all very interesting."

"What do you think? Would you like to come back with Tristan?" she asked.

"I don't know. I'd have to talk to him about it."

"Oh Maya, you seem so shy all of a sudden. Don't be."

"We're all adults," Roderick said.

"No, no, I'm not being shy," I said. "I'm just not sure I'm ready for something like this."

"Oh, come now. Surely you are. You were curious enough to come back here with us," Maddie said. "You're just a little nervous. Don't worry, I was too, my first time." She sat on one couch and patted the cushion next to her for me to sit. "Why don't we just get to know each other first—just the three of us? It'll be easier for you, I think."

"No, Maddie. I'm sorry. But this isn't for me. Not yet anyway. What time is it anyway? I need to get back and meet Tristan."

When Roderick stepped up behind me and put his hands on my shoulders, I cringed. "You have plenty of time. Relax." His grip and his tone set my senses on alert.

"No. I need to go. Now."

Maddie stood up and walked up to me. "Loosen up, Maya," she whispered. Then she put her hand on my breast and leaned forward to kiss me.

"Stop it!" I said, swatting her hand away. "I said I'm leaving."

Maddie looked past me at Roderick. She nodded her head to the left.

I don't know what Roderick was doing behind me, but he took her nod as direction. He wrapped both arms around me and picked me up, carrying me further into the room. I tried to wiggle my arms free and escape his grasp, but it was futile. I kicked back at him repeatedly until one of my spiky heels made contact with his shin.

"Aghh!" He dropped me onto the floor. "Bitch! You made me bleed!"

"Good! Don't fuckin' touch me like that again!" I ran toward the doorway to escape, but Maddie stepped in the way. I pushed her to the side, but then Roderick grabbed me from behind. I flailed my arms and legs trying to make contact with him, but he had embraced me tighter this time with a bear hug grasp and I could barely breathe. He threw me onto my back on the table, knocking the wind from my chest. Maddie grabbed one arm and fastened it to the table before I knew what was happening.

When I reached over with my other arm to unfasten it, Roderick sat on my upper legs, pinning me down. He then held my free arm down so Maddie could fasten it in.

"Get off me! Untie me, you fuckin' assholes. Who the fuck do you think you are!"

CHAPTER 14

They ignored me.

"I thought you gave her the drink," Maddie said to Roderick.

"I did. She drank the whole thing. I don't know why it's not working yet."

"It better. She needs to be more compliant."

"I don't know. I kind of like it feisty like this."

"Roderick, we don't want her to remember any of it. It better work."

"It will, Madeleine. It will. It just might take a little longer."

I was so glad I tossed the drink. And I wasn't going to mention it lest they give me whatever the hell they tried to drug me with. What an idiot I was to come here. My impulsive decisions foiling me once again.

"Madeleine? Roderick?" I said. *"The Fall of the House of Usher*. Those aren't even your fuckin' names. Who the fuck are you? And what do you want from me?"

"We told you already," Roderick said. "We want to play.

And you want to play too, or you wouldn't have come back with us."

"I want to leave. *Now.*"

"But we haven't even started yet," Maddie said, running her hand across my breast.

"Don't touch me, psycho."

She laughed. Roderick said to her, "I'm going to start a fire." Then he turned to me. "I love to fuck in front of a roaring fire."

Fuck! I'm so screwed. What the hell is wrong with me? Why would I leave with two strangers?

"I have no desire to fuck you, Roderick, tonight or any night."

"Don't act so prim," Maddie said. "We saw you dancing pretty close with that blond guy the other night. Looked as if you had a fight with your guy about it, too."

Eek. Busted. But it was more than just a fight. My heart was broken. No, my entire soul felt crushed that night.

"I don't care what it looked like to you. *I don't want to have sex with either one of you. Ever.* This is me saying *no*. No, no, no, no, no. Is that clear?"

"Don't worry, sweetie. You won't remember it." Maddie pinched my nipple.

"Get your nasty little hands off me!" I bucked on the table to jar her hand off.

Roderick said, "Fuck yeah. I like her feisty like that. Even though she hurt my leg. Dammit, it's still bleeding. Let me just get the fire going."

Roderick put some logs into the fireplace. I watched as he moved kindling and logs around to place them where he wanted. Maddie slithered her fingers over my thighs, moving dangerously higher.

"Don't touch me again, you twisted fuck."

She smiled coldly as she pulled back. "Careful or I'll get a gag." She then twisted a nipple through my dress. "But maybe you'll like that."

This is bad, Maya. You need to stop reacting to what they do and think of what you can do next to get out of this.

I slowed down my breathing to try for some self-control, not one of my strong suits.

Focus. Focus.

What can you do to get out of this mess?

I zoned away from my predicament there on the table and shifted my focus to the fire. I looked past Roderick and into the fireplace, watching where the smoke gathered.

This is what you are good at. Use this strength.

I concentrated on where the smoke gathered, where the heat was most intense.

This might backfire.

As soon as the fire caught on the first log, I propelled the flame out of the fireplace. Before he had time to react, the little flame magnified instantly to reach out and burn one of Roderick's hands.

"Fuck!" he screamed and ran out of the room. The sound of a faucet being turned on was followed my more swears.

"What happened?" Maddie asked, following him. "Are you okay?"

"I don't know," he said. "The goddamn fire blew up at me. Is it under control now?"

She came back into the room and looked at the fire, which had settled back into a cozy little flame. "Yeah. It's fine. You sure you didn't just fall into it?"

"I'm sure," he said. He cursed some more. "This is bad. I think I need to go to the emergency room."

Maddie rolled her eyes. "What are we going to do with her? Just when we got her on the table."

"Leave her here. She's not going anywhere any time soon. The drugs will work for hours."

"Can't you just go by yourself? I'll stay with Maya. I'm sure I can find ways to keep us entertained until you get back."

"I can't drive. It's my fuckin' right hand—and it burns like hell! You need to drive me."

Maddie pouted, looked me over, and then said, "Don't worry. We'll be back soon."

"You can't just leave me here tied up!"

"You'll be fine." Raising her hand, she then blew me a kiss.

Ugh. Gross.

She threw some ashes to smother the flames and exited the room. In another minute, the sound of the front door closing signaled they'd left.

Okay, now what? You got them out of here, but you're still tied up.

I scanned the room again. Maybe I could find something to help me undo these fastenings.

No, nothing.

Think, Maya. What can you do?

If I was really strong, I could break through the fastenings. If I was really flexible, I could do some Houdini trick, maybe.

What could *I* do? I looked into the fire as I thought about how to get out of here.

That's it. The answer is right in front of me.

What I was about to do was dangerous. It could in fact kill me if I didn't do it right. And I'd never done anything like it before. In fact, it was the opposite of what I'd been trained to do as a firefighter.

It could backfire and I'd go up in flames.

Literally.

But I couldn't just lie there waiting for some pissed-off captors to return to do what they wanted with me on this damn table.

Taking a few deep breaths to clear my head, I focused on the embers beneath the ash. I practiced with some small exercises. Made tiny flames rise and fall, and funnel—the usual party tricks.

Then, ever so carefully, I encouraged it to grow bigger, beyond the confines of the fireplace and out to the wall facing the street.

It worked.

Yes, keep going now. Go toward the front window. But stay there. Just draw some attention.

The fire roared up and sped along the walls, much quicker than I had intended.

I swallowed, hoping I hadn't made a fatal mistake.

CHAPTER 15

T *ristan*
From the shadows, I saw the couple leave the house. They climbed into a black sedan and drove off.

But where was Maya? Why would she stay alone in a house, presumably their house?

Discomforting sensations crawled up my spine. I rubbed the back of my neck. I didn't like the idea of Maya in there alone and wanted to make sure she was all right.

But what the hell could I do? Ring the front doorbell and say, "Oh, hey, Maya. I was in the neighborhood and I saw you go in here. Just thought I'd say hi."

Yeah, that would go over well. I could just see her freaking out, blue eyes blazing once again. She'd say I was stalking her, she was a grown woman who didn't need someone taking care of her, and to leave her alone.

Did I really want to ruin building something again by being such a suspicious control freak?

So instead, I stood there like a creep and waited. Waited for what, I don't know. I suppose I waited for Maya to come out so I knew she was okay.

But then something I never would have expected happened. Smoke drifted near a window on the far right. Was I seeing things?

I watched more carefully. What the hell was going on in there?

No, that wasn't just smoke. It was fire!

Shit! Maya had to be in there. I never saw her come out.

I ran to the house and tried looking in some windows, but the curtains were all drawn. Then I ran to the front door, lightly tapped the door knob to make sure it wasn't burning. When I tried to turn it, it was locked.

The flames grew.

Fuck. I had to do something.

As I ran to the opposite side of the house, I called 911. I gave the quickest of rundowns while I searched for a rock big enough to cause damage.

"House fire. Caldecott St. White house at far end of cul-de-sac."

I hung up while the operator asked questions. Then I smashed a side window. The sound of breaking glass pierced through the quiet.

"Anybody in here?" I called.

"Tristan?" Maya called from far off. "Is that you?"

"Maya, are you okay? Where are you?"

"I'm in the room at the end of the hall. Come quick. And be careful."

I broke the rest of the window so I could climb through into the living room, and then I ran down the hall. Seeing Maya tied to a table in a room filled with flames kicked me into action.

"Tristan," she whispered. "You came. How did you find me?"

"Not now, Maya. Let me untie you." I fumbled with the

restraints, which were some sort of Velcro-and-metal combination.

After I undid the first one, I asked, "What did they do to you?" But when I looked up at Maya, her eyes were closed. Her lips barely moved but she was saying something. What was she saying?

The flames in the front window, the ones that signaled to me to call for help, were—receding. They were pulling back.

Was she controlling it?

Not wanting to interrupt her trance, I quietly loosened the remaining fastenings. She was free.

The sound of sirens approached.

"Maya, let's get out of here," I said.

"No. I have to get it back under control," she said.

"Maya, no! You're not staying in a burning house. Maybe you can control it, maybe not. We're not staying here to find out. Come with me now!"

I grabbed her hand and we ran down the hall. The closest door I saw led from the kitchen out to the back of the house. Not sure if she'd break free and try to go back to the fire, I made sure she walked out before me.

I didn't have to worry about her running back. Once she broke free of the house and heard the sirens, she ran as if she was being chased by someone. Once we were far enough away from the burning house, I stopped running.

"Maya, I need to tell you something."

She looked frantic, as if adrenaline was telling her to keep running. "What, Tristan? We need to get away from there."

"I fuckin' love you." I put both hands on either side of her head and crushed down on her lips with my own. Finally, her itchy feet stopped moving.

"Oh, Tristan. You never stop surprising me," she said. "I love you, too." She kissed me again. "Now let's go. I'll explain everything. And then we can talk to the authorities later.

177

Right now, I want to get as far away from that house and those people as I can."

She grabbed my hand and we ran from the approaching sirens.

MAYA

What a crazy turn of events.

"Madeleine" and "Roderick" were arrested. I escaped an arson charge. I mean, come on, who would believe it anyway if I confessed to setting a fire with my mind while I was tied up? I'd be locked up forever. Plus, in my opinion it was self-defense. Perhaps they couldn't live in their house for a while, but with the charges they were facing, they might be spending time in another house for many years.

When Tristan and I were alone again, I explained the rationale behind my bad decision of going with them.

"I thought it might be something hot we could try together. I mean, doesn't every guy want to see his girl with another girl? But I changed my mind as soon as I got in there. I only want you."

Tristan shook his head. "Oh Maya. I don't want to share you with anyone."

I raised an eyebrow. "So, you're saying you don't want to see me with another girl?"

His eyes widened. "All I want right now is you. You and only you. In my life, in my bed." He placed his hand over his chest. "And in my heart."

I wrapped my arms around his neck and smiled. "Great answer."

Tristan and I built our relationship over the next few weeks, taking things much more slowly.

As we walked hand in hand along the ocean, he said,

"Let's focus on us first. I don't care about any spells or potions or figuring out if we were meant to be together in some other, deeper way."

"What about the darkness?"

"You'll always be my light. In every way." He kissed me on the forehead. "It's time I take you on some proper dates."

He kept his word. We went on actual dates. They were as secluded as possible, but they were dates nonetheless. We went to restaurants and the movies. As long as Tristan focused on me, he could block out external distractions. I didn't mind—in fact, I loved the attention. One mild day, we even took an enclosed boat out on the Atlantic.

Being alone out on the open water was too much for us to resist. We ended up entangled in each other's arms as we rekindled that attraction that led us together at Vamps to begin with.

"I missed you so much, Maya. I missed *this* so much. Being with you."

"I know exactly what you mean."

We spent Christmas afternoon with Tristan's parents and rang in the New Year at a big bash at Vamps. After several weeks of spending time together as a couple, I asked, "Are you ready to try again? Back in the lab?"

Tristan appeared hesitant at first and then he soldiered on. "Yes," he said, "I don't think we need the lab, though."

I raised my eyebrows.

"Seeing how you focused on the fire at, you know—*their* —house, it gave me an idea."

"Oh no, Tristan. What do you have in mind?"

"A camping trip. Out under the stars. And a campfire."

"Are you kidding me? It's winter. In New England. People don't camp now, they ski."

"Some do with the right equipment. Besides, it's a mild

179

winter. Global warming, unfortunately. And I'll keep you warm."

"I'm not sleeping in a tent in January. Surely that doesn't have to be part of the plan."

"We can get a cabin."

"A heated cabin."

"A heated cabin. Wimp."

"I'd rather be a warm wimp than a freezing fool."

"Come here, my warm wimp," he said, pulling me into his arms. "Show some love to your fool."

"You mean *freezing* fool."

"How about devoted fool?"

"I like it."

"Me too."

He kissed me and ran his hands down my body.

"Before you get too carried away," I said, "tell me about your cockamamie plan."

The fact that Tristan could lure me to the woods on a January day was a testament to how crazy I was about him. But at least we had a cozy log cabin stocked with food and drink we had picked up at a gourmet market.

We laid out a baguette, cheese spreads, tomato, cucumber, and all kinds of fruit on the table. And to go with it, a bottle of red wine.

"This weekend is starting to look up," I said. "Aren't you glad we're not roughing it?"

Tristan looked over to the bed. "I'm looking forward to christening that bed. But sleeping with you in a tent sounded like fun too."

"Does it now? I can pretty much promise you that will never happen."

He raised his eyebrows. "Never?"

"Okay, maybe in the summer. But definitely not now."

"I'm going to book a weekend in July before we leave so we'll have to come back."

"Oh, Tristan. Planning seven months ahead. Aren't you the optimist about our relationship."

"No more doubts, Maya. I'm yours. And I hope you're mine."

"Absolutely."

We walked through the woods that afternoon, seeing if we could find animals or animal tracks. Then Tristan said we should get back to start a fire so we could try his plan.

He set up kindling for a fire and fumbled to get it started.

"Allow me," I said. I'd been working on developing my connection with fire since the incident and could now direct my energy to spark a small candle-sized flame.

"Showoff," he teased.

"Can I show off for you later?"

"Only if you take special requests."

"Sure. What will it be, Mr. Stone?"

"You on top. Oral. Missionary. Doggy style. You name it."

"Let's shake on it." We shook hands. "Now tell me why you brought me here."

"I thought being out in nature among the other elements instead of a basement might help you with your gift. I mean, there's air, earth, water, and now fire here—not potions in some basement."

"Oh. Good thinking," I said. "But how will this help you?"

"I don't know. But I think you're the key. And you might be able to concentrate better out here."

"Fair enough. What do you want me to do?"

"Focus on the fire."

I watched the fire flicker and concentrated on the dancing flames. I fixed my gaze on one color after another, clearing my head of clutter. I don't know how long we sat there, but at some point all the junk that usually occupied my head disappeared. The world appeared wide open and clear, the sky infinite.

"Oh my God," Tristan said. "Unbelievable."

"What is it?" I said, wanting to look at him but not wanting to break my connection to the fire.

"Your light. It's magnificent. It's exploded into thousands of little colors. Like a rainbow in a diamond."

"Really?"

"I feel something in me too. Whatever it is, I feel it."

"What is it, Tristan?"

"Some sort of energy, I think. Keep doing what you're doing."

I stayed in that trance-like state for several minutes where my mind was clear and pure. But then I had to look away and once I did, I felt exhausted.

Tristan said, "Whatever you did was powerful. It's as if a weight has been lifted off of me. As if a burden has been lifted off my soul."

Tristan

Maya and I walked into a café the next morning to pick up coffees and bagels. As I waited in line, I scanned the people sitting at the tables. The darkness around them had changed. I tilted my head, fascinated by the transformation.

She nudged my arm. "You're staring at them," she whispered.

I bent my head and whispered back, "Can't help it. They're surrounded by colors. Not darkness and shadows."

Maya's eyes widened. "Really?"

When the cashier called us, we moved ahead. After we received our breakfast, we exited the café.

"Why do you think that happened?" Maya asked.

I shook my head. "I'm still trying to figure that out. Whatever you did last night must have broken through some barrier in my mind."

We headed toward the sound of the waves lapping the shore. When we reached the sandy beach, we removed our shoes. The scent of ocean and sea life tingled my nostrils and I inhaled more deeply. With the fragrance of the French vanilla coffee as well, it was a bouquet of pleasing aromas.

The morning sea breeze cooled our skin. The cup warmed my hands and I alternated between them to offset the brisk air. I took a sip of the hot coffee while looking out to the sea. What a perfect morning. I couldn't think of a better way to start the day with my girl.

Well, after a morning quickie, of course.

The sun rose over the ocean in a brilliant orange that danced with a fiery reflection on the ripples of waves. A bright morning signaling hope on a new day.

While sipping our coffee and nibbling the scones as we walked through the sand, we threw out ideas as to what might have happened last night.

"The only person I can think of who might have an explanation is my mother. Would you go over there with me today?"

"Of course," Maya said.

That afternoon, I drove us to Salem. Over a quiche in the courtyard, I explained the new phenomenon with colors and not feeling so world-weary.

My mother leaned back in her chair and smiled. "I've always thought you could be a healer, Tristan. Maybe Maya's gift helped you tap into it."

"How does seeing colors make me a healer?"

"Auras, maybe. Energy?" She raised her hand, palm up. "Your great-grandfather could see something in people that most of us can't. He used it to help people. Heal them."

From the seat beside me, Maya said, "That's amazing."

183

More questions rose. "How?"

"Maybe he knew how to move energy. He never really explained it. People came to see him when they were feeling distraught and he had the ability to make them feel a little less so. A little more optimistic to face whatever they had ahead of them."

I humphed, not knowing what to say.

We didn't say much over the next couple of minutes as we ate, likely all considering what my mother had said.

She leaned forward. "Tristan, are you willing to try something, with a volunteer?"

"What? Try what? With whom?"

She called out into the hallway. "Charlotte, come here please."

Charlotte appeared moments later. "Yes, Mrs. Stone?"

"Remember how we were talking about Tristan? About how he just needed to break through?"

"I do."

"We think he has." She looked at me and back at Charlotte. "I'm wondering if you both will try something."

I tilted my head with skepticism. "Mother…"

"Hear me out," she said, raising a hand. "You know that Charlotte is still in mourning for her husband. She's been in pain for far too long. We've been talking about how she needs to move on with her life, but she's not sure how to begin."

After exchanging a glance with Maya, I answered. "I have a feeling you have some crazy idea in mind that involves me."

"It's not crazy," Mother said, and then conceded. "Okay, maybe it's a bit odd. But nothing would ever have been invented if people hadn't had a few untraditional ideas and had been willing to try things."

"True." I nodded.

"What I think you should do is sit with Charlotte, hold

her hand and try to connect with her. Maybe send some positive energy her way." She turned to Charlotte. "Are you still willing to try something like this?"

"I'm willing to try anything, Mrs. Stone. The sadness I feel, it's not a good way to live."

She turned back to me. "Tristan?"

I scanned the three women before me. Maya's eyes twinkled with excitement. "I don't think you ladies would let me say no at this point even if I tried."

Mother smiled. "Great. It's settled. Here, Charlotte, come sit down. Tristan, take her hands."

"What do I do?"

"Focus your energy on her. Send her positive energy."

I gazed at the colors surrounding Charlotte. Dark blue, light blue and the darkness within. I tried to focus on her.

"I can't," I said. "I need Maya."

"I'm right here." Maya squeezed my thigh from beside me.

"Let's go outside and light the fire," I suggested

We retreated into the garden and took our seats. Maya focused on the fire. I fixed my gaze on her lightness, her luminous colors, until I was filled with a positive energy. Closing my eyes and letting it extend to all parts of my body, I then willed the energy to move toward Charlotte.

The strangest sensation occurred. A physical presence actually left my body and headed into hers.

What the hell is going on?

I don't know how much time had passed, but when the energy transfer had passed, I turned to Charlotte.

She glanced around with a surprised expression. Then she smiled. "Mr. Stone, I don't know what you've done, but I felt it. I actually feel lighter. The ache, the sorrow isn't so heavy."

"What about when you think of your husband?" Mother asked.

Charlotte furrowed her brows. "I still miss him. Mourn him. But it's different. The grief is part of me and always will be, but I don't think it will hold me back from living my life any longer." She exhaled. "Much better than I've felt in months. Thank you. Thank you so much."

The dark blue and light blue that had surrounded her met and created a blend between them. And the darkness within her was smaller.

Darkness. There was someone else I knew who had a darkness hiding deep within.

"Tristan!" Mother exclaimed, clasping her hands. "I knew it. I always believed in you!"

"What does this mean?" I turned to her.

"It means you have begun to tap into your gifts. It isn't something that happens overnight, but is something you can develop. Think of all the people you could help. Is this something you want to do?"

"My life has lacked meaning for so long that I would gladly do something of value. But I don't want to try this alone. Excuse us, please, Mother. Charlotte."

They left the garden. I walked over to Maya and took her hands. "If you're with me, I'll try anything. Will you stay with me, Maya?"

She looked down before looking at me with earnest blue eyes and said, "I've been with you since our first night together. I'll always be here."

I kissed her in appreciation, lifting her off the ground.

When our lips parted, I said, "Let me look at you a moment."

"Yes. Why?

"Remember how I told you about the darkness I saw buried deep inside you?"

"Yes," she whispered.

"I don't see it anymore. It's gone."

"Naturally. You're in my life." She smiled. "In case you didn't notice, you're also the light to my dark."

"Of course not. I'm just an idiot," I teased.

She smiled. "No, I'm the idiot. You're the dumbass. Remember?"

"Oh yeah." I grinned. "Now that we've started working together again, there's one thing I want to do."

"Let me guess, something that involves leather. Maybe a pink wig?"

"You're on the right track," I said.

She nodded in acquiescence. "What do you want to do?"

"Go back to the cemetery."

CHAPTER 16

We left my parent's house in Salem and drove back to Cat's Cove. At dusk, we walked hand-in-hand from my loft to the cemetery. When I saw the familiar shadows slink around tombstones, I gripped Maya's hand more tightly.

She gave me a reassuring smile. "It's going to be fine."

Once we settled at a spot at a safe distance from the trees, Maya pulled out a candle. She closed her eyes and her lips moved as she concentrated. When she reopened them, a flame flickered from the candle. Seconds later, a breeze from the ocean extinguished it. She repeated the action, but the same outcome resulted.

"This is going to be difficult here with the breeze," she said.

I glanced at our surroundings. "Put it behind one of the tombstones to block the breeze."

She flashed me a brilliant smile. "Genius." With a tilt of her head, she pointed at me, "More than just a pretty face, my friend."

"More than just a friend, my pretty lover," I replied.

Her eyes sparkled. "Yes, lover."

We moved behind a crypt, which was more than sufficient to block the breeze. Maya returned her attention to the candle. Once she'd established a steady flame, she practiced making it rise. It did so about four times the normal flame on a candle.

"Let's focus again," she said. "Me on the flame, you on my light."

I concentrated, fixing my gaze on her unique glow. Something strange zipped through me. It was her energy. How I knew this or how it worked, I don't know. Maybe she gained energy from the flame and then I gained positive healing energy from her.

Once I saw the colors shimmer like mother of pearl, I said, "Okay, I've got it."

The graveyard appeared like a different world than the one I'd just seen.

"Holy shit, Maya. I wish you could see this. It's unreal."

The shadows that had crept around the stones when we first arrived, the same shadows that Maya drove away or masked with her light, were now more visible.

"What is it?"

"They're not dark, slithering shadows anymore. I now see more colorful areas—like light and energy."

"What do you think they are?" she asked.

I shook my head. "Spirits?"

"Can you talk to them?"

I quit staring out into the graveyard to look at Maya. "What am I supposed to say? 'Hi, are you a spirit?'"

"Don't be sarcastic, Tristan." Raising her chin, she said. "Not when we're having a breakthrough."

"Okay. Sorry. Seriously, what do you think I should do?"

"Um, I'm thinking," she said. She started pacing in a figure eight. "This is really weird. But it kind of makes sense. Think about it. Your great-grandfather could see auras; your mother is a medium. Somehow you've inherited some of each of their gifts and developed your own."

I shook my head out of incredulity. It was crazy, but in a way it made sense.

Maya kept pacing. "If they are spirits, they might be stuck here. Or lost. Why else would they creep around the graveyard? Maybe you need to send them positive energy. To help guide them."

I gave her a doubtful look, but resisted asking, where the hell am I supposed to guide them? She did find some sensible explanation of this wacky situation so I held my comments.

The colors surrounding us entranced me. "Okay, I'll try."

I inhaled deeply, trying to take in as much of Maya's positive energy as I could. Then I willed it out toward the shapes and colors around me.

Seconds pass, but nothing happened. *Well, that was interesting.* I bit the sarcastic comment back, since there was no need to release my frustrations on her. As I was about to let go of the connection, a light-blue shape caught my eye. It was in the back of the graveyard. I squinted to get a better look. It was oval in shape, but as it floated along the ground of the cemetery, its edges reshaped as if stretched, one side clinging for the earth, while the other reached for the heavens.

My mouth fell open as I tracked it. Soon, it pulled away from the soil and floated up. As it ascended over the graveyard, the blue color faded. First, it turned white and then translucent. Only the outline was visible.

And then it disappeared.

I snapped my mouth shut. "Unreal."

"What is it?"

"It's amazing. I'll explain later."

"I don't know how much longer I can do this, Tristan. It's draining me."

When I glanced at her, "Hold on a little longer, please."

Encouraged, I directed the energy toward another shadow, this one orange. By focusing on this one shadow rather than the entire graveyard, the process repeated much more quickly this time.

"It's working!"

"What's working?"

"I don't know exactly. But they're moving—moving on, I think."

I focused on the last one as quickly as I could. Finally, no signs of life were left in the graveyard except for Maya and me. Peace at last.

I let go of the energy transfer and turned to Maya.

Her face was pale and covered with a slight sheen. She sighed and then fainted.

I ran to her. "Maya!"

She didn't respond. Shit. When I assessed her vital signs, she was all right. What could I do for her? We couldn't stay in the graveyard. If someone happened on us and found me with an unconscious woman, it would be bad. And I couldn't bring her to the hospital. I couldn't explain what had caused her to pass out.

Shit. I had to get her to my loft where she could rest. I'd call my mother and see what we should do. I carried Maya out of the cemetery, hoping no cops drove by in the short distance to my place.

Maya

When I woke, the scent of fresh brewed coffee reached me. I opened my eyes. The spectacular view of the ocean meant I had to be in Tristan's loft. When I turned my head, I spotted him in the kitchen.

"What happened?" I asked.

He smiled and walked over and sat on the bed. "You passed out."

I remembered the exhaustion. "I wonder why."

He shrugged. "My mother thought you released too much of your energy and needed to rest to restore it."

I nodded. More events of last night returned to me. "Tell me what happened with you. What did you see?"

"I saw colors floating through the graveyard rather than shadows. They reflected light. When I directed our energy toward them, they rose into the sky and disappeared."

"I've seen a lot of things, baby." I raised my brows. "But that's some freaky-ass shit."

"No. It was a positive experience," he said.

He walked to the coffee pot and poured some into a mug. When he handed it to me, I inhaled the hazelnut brew and curled both hands around it to warm my palms.

"Tristan, I wonder if you even need me anymore?"

"What? What are you talking about?"

"I mean to tap into the energy or whatever it is that you can do."

"You're the key, Maya. Of course I need you."

"But maybe I was just the key to break through. You might be able to tap into the energy yourself now."

"You're talking crazy this morning. Here, drink some coffee."

"I'm serious, Tristan. You should try it on your own one day."

"Okay, maybe." He sat down next to me on the bed and drank some coffee. "I hope that's not your excuse to try to slip away. You know I like having you with me. Just being near you brings me comfort."

"Oh, you're so sweet. And you make a killer cup of coffee. Guess I'll stick around for a little bit," I teased.

"You better not go anywhere anytime soon. In fact, you should take it easy today. Tonight, I have a surprise for you."

"Ah, I know about you and your surprises," I teased. "What is it—something kinky?"

"You are such a sexy little vixen." He kissed my mussed-up hair. "But that's not what I was planning. Not at first, anyhow. Come to Vamps tonight. And dress hot."

"Don't I always?" I tilted my head.

"Yes. You could make a pair of overalls look smokin'. But tonight is special."

I found the black dress with the red Asian accents that I'd worn the second night I met Tristan. So many things had happened since that night.

When I saw Byron, he said, "You're practically a fixture here. What do you and Mr. Stone do anyway?"

The experiments and the sex came to mind. He'd get the sex part; the experiments, not so much. I gave him the look. "Do I *really* have to explain that to you?"

"Ugh, please don't. He's my boss, you know. I don't want to hear about his sex life. Gross."

"I assure you there's nothing gross about it. In fact, it's kind of—"

"La la la la la." Byron covered his ears. "I can't hear you. I'm singing."

"For a bouncer at an underground club, you're kind of a prude."

"No gay guy wants to hear about straight people having sex."

"I wasn't going to tell you details, Byron. Jeez. I was just going to say he makes me very happy."

"Ewww," he replied. "It's like my mom telling me my dad is good in bed."

I pinched his arm in a playful manner. "I'm not old enough to be your mom."

"Yeah, but he's my boss."

"Fine." I raised my chin. "Interpret it how you will. Now if you'll excuse me, I'm going to find the guy who gives me great—*happiness*." I gave Byron a sassy smile and entered the club.

Tristan met me at the bar rather than down in the lab where I usually found him.

"Have a drink, Maya. We need to celebrate."

"Our discovery? How we can work together?" I asked.

"That and other things."

When the bartender came over, I said, "I'll have a Tempting Fate." After all, look at all the good things that happened since the first night I tried one of those.

"The surprise is coming up. Look on stage."

Band members came on with their instruments. "Oh my God! Velvet Cocks. I love this band!"

He shook his head and laughed. "What a band name. You know they just wanted hot girls like you to go around saying 'I love Velvet Cocks!'"

"I love Velvet Cocks!" I echoed with a laugh.

"I know," he said. "I've seen your music collection. Who buys records anymore these days?"

"This girl," I said, pointing both thumbs at my chest.

Tristan shook his head. "You can have your entire music collection stored digitally and you still have bulky vinyl?"

"One day I'll let you experience the magic—if you're good."

"I'm always good—except when I'm bad."

"I like it when you're bad—in bed."

Tristan opened his mouth in mock horror. "Are you saying I'm bad in bed?"

"No. Of course not." I gave him a playful punch on his

arm. "You're frickin' awesome in bed. You know what I mean, Tristan!"

"Just teasing." He nodded toward the stage. "I booked them for you. You haven't seen a live band here yet. I wanted your first experience to be unforgettable."

"Hey there, stranger." The woman's voice from behind me made me turn.

"Nike! What are you doing here?" I gave her a giant hug. She was standing next to Michel; I recognized him as the guy she turned tongue-tied with the night of the fire. Damn, I forgot how good-looking he was. He had light brown hair down to his chin and intense blue eyes. Not my type, but I could see why Nike would go ga-ga over him.

And he was a fucking vampire. Holy crap. I tried not to stare at him. Besides, if the Hollywood renditions were true, he might be able to entrance me or some shit.

"Maya," he said with a slight bow of his head.

When he spoke, I peeked to search for fangs. No signs. "Welcome back, Michel."

"It's good to be back," he said.

"Why don't you ladies have fun out there?" Tristan said. "Michel and I will be at the bar."

Confused, I asked, "You know each other?"

"Of course," Tristan said. "We have done business together, remember?" He motioned around the club that Tristan bought from Michel after the fire.

"But, that's while Nike and Michel were overseas, I thought."

"He got in touch when they came back to the U.S." He kissed me and said, "Have fun with your girlfriend."

It didn't take long for that to happen. Nike and I jumped around like crazy, singing our favorite songs along with the Velvet Cocks, or VC as they were known in more PC crowds. Their logo had a rooster wearing a smoking jacket with the letters VC in a fancy scroll font. Fun, cheeky bastards.

While we danced again for the first time in over a year, I thought it was as if Nike had never left. And became some sort of creature of the night, if that's what she was. She was still Nike and I was still me.

After a set, the singer said, "This next song goes out to Maya, a very special lady, from her eternal admirer."

Nike and I looked at each other. Her eyes were wide, reflecting the self-conscious horror she'd feel if Michel did this to her. But not me, I enjoyed the spotlight. When I beamed, she smiled back.

I turned back to see Tristan at the bar, grinning. For Tristan to even be out here socializing, it was a big thing.

The singer Leggy Bones began with a soft croon of *#1 Crush* by Garbage, an ode to an obsessive, all-consuming type of love. I stood there gaping like an idiot. Did Tristan really feel so much for me? It was only after the seductive intro, when the guitarist Chee Keydood led the band with a punk rift, that I regained my composure and danced around for the rest of the song. They played it hard and heavy—one of my favorite bands jamming out to a song chosen from my favorite guy—dedicated to *me*! I reveled in the moment, dancing without a care.

Leggy motioned to Nike and me. "Come on up here for the next song."

I climbed up without reservation, but figured Nike would decline. To my surprise, she climbed next to me on the stage.

Hmm, maybe Michel was good for her after all. With her the more reserved one and him outgoing, they were the opposite pair of Tristan and me. I couldn't be with someone as flighty and spontaneous as I was—it would drive me insane. Tristan had a way of grounding me.

Leggy brought us over to him with the mic. "I think we all

know this one. We put our spin on it. Come on, everyone now, sing along."

Velvet Cocks launched into their version of *Witchcraft*, punk-rock style—quick, hard and heavy. Nike and I were on either side of Leggy, singing along. I caught Tristan's eye and smiled as he watched me from the bar. He had a twinkle in his dark eyes now; the haunted look was gone. He raised his glass and nodded.

After gallivanting on stage for another song, Nike and I joined the guys at the bar.

"Let's all have a drink," Tristan said.

I looked around our little group as we drank a round of a Fateful Night. A vampire, a woman experiencing vampire-like symptoms, a man who could see auras or energy, and a woman who could manipulate fire. "If this isn't the motley-est of crews, I don't know what is."

Everyone laughed. I couldn't have been happier. I had my guy, my best friend, and one of my favorite bands—in my favorite club.

"Thanks for inviting us here tonight," Nike said to Tristan.

"My pleasure. It's great to see old friends catching up as if no time has passed between them."

A pang of sadness went through me. Had he ever had friends? Probably not.

"How long are you two sticking around?" I asked them.

"Indefinitely," Michel answered. "I still own the rock-climbing gym, although it's suffered from mismanagement since I've been gone. I'm hoping Nike will help me whip it back into shape."

When Nike beamed at him, he gazed back with pure affection in his eyes. I had no doubt that what they felt for each other was real. I vowed to stop feeling angry at Michel for monopolizing my best friend—and leading her to become some sort of creature of the night. If she was happy, then I was happy for her. Or, I would be, eventually.

Michel turned back to Tristan and me. "Perhaps you should come check it out one day. It's a great workout."

"Uhhh—" I began. "I don't know about that."

"Oh, come on, Maya." Tristan nudged me. "It'll be fun. Something new."

Was this the same guy who avoided people? He certainly was trying new things for me.

"Okay. Maybe," I said. "I warn you, though. I'm not very athletic. Just because I can shake my booty here doesn't mean I'll have any sort of coordination climbing a wall."

"You'll do just fine," Michel said.

"And I'll catch you if you fall," Tristan added.

"Falling may be involved? I might have to change my mind already."

Tristan ignored me. "We'll be there soon."

"What about the firehouse, Nike?" I asked, hoping she'd give it some thought.

"Let's see how it goes," she said. "It's easier to start with the rock climbing gym since Michel owns it. I'd need to come up with a damn good reason why I left the firehouse and an even better one for why I'd want the night shift. I wouldn't want to rush into things here and have it all go up in flames." She winked.

We all laughed at her choice of words.

"Good point," I added.

Michel and Nike began canoodling at the bar so Tristan and I moved closer to the stage to watch the band finish their set. After they finished playing, I turned to Tristan.

"Do you notice anything different about Nike and Michel?" I asked.

He glanced at them and back at me. "Nothing stands out. Why?"

Now wasn't the time to get into the Nike situation, especially not without her consent. "She's my best friend and I worry about her."

"She looks happy, Maya," Tristan said. "No need to worry about her right now."

It was true. She had a smile on her face as she listened to whatever Michel said.

"You're right. Thank you, Tristan. What a fantastic night. Everything you did was especially sweet. Very thoughtful."

"Thank you. For everything. Do you know how different I feel knowing I can make a difference in the world, rather than hiding from it in a basement? I feel like a new man. And it's all because of you."

I didn't know what to say.

"I want to try things I've avoided all these years. And one of the first things I want to try is rock climbing." When I groaned, he said, "You're coming with me."

"If you insist," I teased.

"I know we took things too quickly in the beginning and I don't want to do that again. The last several weeks with us taking things slow while we 'date' have been phenomenal. But I do want you with me as much as possible. What do you think about moving in with me? Living in the loft?"

My heart pounded. Then my hands turned clammy.

Holy crap! This was a big commitment. Moving in with him? Am I ready? Can I do it? I've been living on my own for so long. How would it work with me sharing my space with someone? Would I be giving up my independence? Focus, Maya, breathe.

"I don't know, Tristan. That's a big proposal to consider."

"No pressure. Just putting it out there. Think about it when you're ready."

"Thanks. I will. You know I tend to make spontaneous decisions." I gave him a knowing smile.

"I've been finding out about your impulsive actions the

hard way," he said, leaning his forehead against mine. "It's one of your most charming—and infuriating—traits."

"You know what they say," I said. "Love me—love all of me."

"I do love you, Maya. All of you." He ran a hand down my side, settling into a protective hold on my lower back. "Every last inch of you."

"I love you, too, Tristan." I kissed him softly.

"Forget about it right now. Listen. The DJ is starting up with your favorite band."

I strained my ears to hear the opening beat of Type O Negative's *Set Me on Fire* and perked up right away.

"Ooh! You must have requested it!"

"One of the perks of being the boss around here," he said. "That and having the most beautiful, crazy, spontaneous, exasperating, kindhearted, spirited, brave, patient, loving woman walk into my club. And into my life."

I smiled. Life had been a whirlwind of emotions the past few months, but I wouldn't change anything. It was all worth it in the end. So what happened in the past, with all our mistakes, helped get us here.

"Come on, let's dance," he said, and took my hand to lead me onto the dance floor. I turned back and caught Nike's eye and she nodded with a knowing look in her eyes. Michel was whispering something into her ear. Probably whatever it was sounded extra seductive in his French accent. And knowing what a sucker she was for it, her insides had probably melted into jelly.

Only a few people were up there right now so we had a wide-open space. Tristan pulled me close and whispered into my ear, "You set me on fire."

I wrapped my arms around him as we swayed to the dark rhythm of the song. It felt so good to be back in his arms. Not dancing with wild abandon to forget a broken heart.

Not dancing with some random guy. But to be here wrapped in Tristan's protective embrace. I rested my head on his chest and sighed softly. How could he evoke feelings of protection, warmth, pure love and a rising desire in me all at once?

"My body is ablaze just thinking of being with you again," I whispered back.

"Don't say things like that or I won't be able to make it to the end of the song without feeling you up out here in front of everyone."

I closed my eyes. His desire intoxicated me. How could I make it through the song without wrapping my legs around his waist and begging for him?

Even through my want, thoughts ran through my head, thoughts about us. Yes, he'd hurt me and I'd hurt him. But all that was behind us right now. We'd learned from our mistakes and maybe that made us stronger going ahead. The future was wide open. Open with possibilities.

You've practically been living with him since you met him. You've spent so many nights with him—and days. It's natural to move on to this next step.

I leaned back to look up at him and saw my own increasing lust reflected in his dark eyes. All the uncertainty about moving forward with him disappeared. How did he have this effect on me?

"I want you right now, Tristan."

He pulled me closer and I felt his erection press against me.

"The feeling is clearly mutual." He pulled away and whispered, "But we'll have to wait until later. Your friend is here tonight. We should spend time with them before we run off to bang like bunnies."

I looked over Tristan's shoulder to the bar. Michel was nuzzling Nike's neck now and her eyes were half-closed.

I laughed. "I don't think we'll have to wait too long."

Tristan looked over at them. "Guess the next question is who's going to run out of here the quickest." He pulled me closer to him and I rested my head on his chest again.

As the song wound down, I pulled back. "Tristan, I've made a decision. I don't need time to think about what I know is right. Yes, I would love to move in with you."

He made some whooping sound and lifted me off the ground. "I do love your impulsive decisions."

"But, I have one condition," I said.

"What is it?" He looked at me with wary eyes.

"Only if we bring the blue scarf home with us."

Tristan laughed. A laugh that used to be so rare with his brooding nature, but one that came out more and more these days. Then he pulled me closer so our lips were only inches apart.

"Our home. I love it," he said. "You're on." He trailed his fingers over my hips. "We need to buy something to make it official."

"And what's that?"

"Another chair for the kitchen table."

An image of the lone chair in his kitchen formed in my mind. The first time I'd seen it, I'd wondered how lonely he must be. Tears of happiness burned behind my eyes, but I squeezed them away.

"Absolutely," I said.

"I have one condition of my own," he said with a decadent glimmer in his eyes.

"What's that?" I asked, breathless. Just as eager to hear the answer as I was to feel his lips on mine.

"I'm tying *you* up first."

Glancing into the dark eyes of the man I loved, I thought of the possibilities that lay ahead. I whispered into his ear, "How about tonight?"

A NOTE FROM THE AUTHOR: I hope you enjoyed Maya and Tristan's romance. They'll be back in later books in the series. I hope you can take a moment to leave a review. Thanks!

Don't miss book 3 in the Underground Encounters series, Ignite. *It begins on the same night that* Fire *ends, but features a different couple, with one of them being the singer for the band, the Velvet Cocks. I had so much fun writing about this band. :D*

Read on for a sneak peak!

EXCERPT OF BOOK 3, IGNITE

Lily Everett won't consider a permanent relationship. When she meets the singer of a rock band at an underground night-club, she's disarmed by his sensual voice and mischievous good looks. After an icy introduction, Lily warms up to Nico's charms.

He's a computer geek by day, and rock star by night. How could she resist such a combination?

But, Lily must keep an emotional distance. Their encounters are hot, but no one would understand her furry little secret. It could be dangerous. Especially during the full moon.

Yet, she might be the one in danger…

Ignite is the next installment in the Underground Encounters series, set in a club that attracts supernatural creatures. Step into Vamps, a thrilling new world of steamy paranormal romance featuring sexy shifters, thirsty vampires, wicked witches, and gorgeous gargoyles.

Chapter One

Lily

We hadn't checked the club's calendar before we went out. I was looking forward to a night of dancing. I didn't go out often, but tonight was a special occasion. So I put on a hot little red-and-black plaid dress, spiky-heeled boots and chunky gold bracelets to go all out. But when we arrived, a loud rock band was playing.

My senses were assaulted by not only the sound, but also the scent of alcohol all around us and sweat coming off people dancing up near the stage. I wasn't used to the night-club scene and it took a few moments for my unusually sensitive senses to adjust.

"Yeah, I guess. They're all right," I agreed, forcing myself not to sulk.

"Give them a chance, Lily. I didn't know you're not into rock, but look at the crowd—they're going nuts. We should join them." She motioned to the people dancing in front of the stage. "Besides, the DJ will come out later and you can shake your fine little booty to some funky-ass music soon."

"Little? Ha! You definitely need glasses," I said. "I'm going to grab a drink first. Want one?"

Ally shook her head. "I'm going to get closer to the stage. See ya in a bit." I watched her as she slunk into the crowd. She was hard not to miss with her dirty-blonde hair in shiny, thick curls hanging down the back of her slinky electric-blue-and-black dress, which definitely stood out among all the people wearing black. Within moments, the crowd filled in the spot into which her tiny body disappeared and I couldn't see her anymore.

Might as well get a drink. When I scanned the menu for something tasty, the Fruits of Temptation caught my eye. Plenty of fruit and plenty more alcohol. Perfect to hit the spot. I found an empty stool under one of the many gargoyle statues mounted at the end of the bar and focused on my drink. Mmm, yummy. I took little sips through a tiny straw. It went down so smooth, but I had better watch it or I'd be on my ass before I knew what happened.

When the crowd starting singing along with the next song, I was distracted from my cocktail. Who wouldn't be— they were chanting the chorus to *Let's Fuck All Over Paris.* What kind of crazy-ass song was this? My ears perked up as I tried to catch lyrics over the crowd.

No money, no hope
But in Paris, I cope
Sad ghosts fill the air
Joy and despair

Then the crowd revved up again to sing the chorus, "Let's fuck all over Paris, Under the moon, under Polaris." I looked for Ally but didn't see her. She was probably one of the jumping figures wearing black up near the front of the stage. Was she singing along too? From this vantage point, I only caught glimpses of the band through the pulsating crowd waving their arms.

I had to admit, Velvet Cocks rocked hard. Real hard. I knew very little about them except they were popular in Boston's underground rock scene. Now hearing them play live at Vamps, I understood how word spread fast. Their energy spilled over into the crowd as they played short original songs and punk-style remakes of classics.

I'd never been to this club Vamps before, never even heard of it. When Ally suggested we go out to celebrate my new promotion, she said, "I know just the place."

I only had time to check out the homepage of the website at work. It introduced itself as an eclectic club with live bands, Goth music, punk, alternative rock, techno and the best music from the vault, whatever that meant. There were no pictures of people on the homepage, only a few images of gargoyles and a spooky-looking sign reading

"Abandon Hope All Ye Who Enter Here." I wasn't sure what to expect.

With the number of gargoyle statues around, from the ones guarding the front door to the ones hanging inside the main dance area, I understood why they were the prominent theme on the website. What struck me was the crowd. They wore all kinds of sexy outfits designed to attract attention, mostly black. Leather pants, catsuits, tight black dresses, schoolgirl outfits and outfits consisting of tiny vinyl straps I assumed were purchased from a fetish shop.

"Wow," was all I could say when we walked in.

"What is it?"

"I've never seen been in a club like this."

Ally said, "Keep an open mind. Don't make judgments, dance without a care in the world, and you'll have the time of your life. I promise you that."

"They way people are dressed. Just—wow."

"You're just wow. And I bet you're a closet freak." "Ha. Hardly. What you see is what you get, baby." She laughed. "Your outfit doesn't leave much the imagination tonight." "You said dress slutty. This is the best I could come up with."

"I know. I know. You look great."

I tried to keep an open mind as I listened to the band. They finished the song about fucking in Paris on a heavy rift and the singer said, "This next song goes out to Maya, a very special lady, from her eternal admirer."

When he spoke, I detected a slight accent, maybe English, which wasn't very noticeable when he sang.

Damn, that dedication was sweet. It must be nice to have someone so into you they'd request a singer to send a shout out to you declaring their feelings. I quickly ran through the guys I'd dated the last few years. Not a chance any of them would ever take that initiative. They were all too emotionally cut off to ever reveal something as personal as feelings. Then again, I wasn't exactly professing any kind of eternal love either. Definitely not in the way this admirer was professing for this Maya. In fact, with my exes, I'd insisted we keep things casual. My dual nature demanded the physical interaction. Bad kitty was often in heat.

But that was my hang-up. No guy would be able to handle my secret.

My thoughts were distracted as I strained to hear the opening of the song. He sang so softly at first I barely made out the lyrics. Then his croon turned into a seductive opening of a song I recognized. *#1 Crush* by Garbage, an admittance of obsessive love. How the hell did he make it sound so tormented and yet so damn sexy all at once?

I had to get a better look and see this guy who was exacting complete control over the crowd. He had them worked up in a frenzy during the last song and now they had settled into a hypnotic sway as they listened to him sing with such intense longing. He delivered it with such a painful croon, almost haunted. That's when I finally caught a glimpse of him.

Holy hell.

I was not expecting someone so—so—like him.

He was wearing a plaid green-and-black cap, but I saw his dark brown hair was cut close to his scalp. He looked so young and innocent at the same time. I pegged him to be in his late twenties. Maybe my age or a couple of years younger than me since I was about to celebrate the first of many twenty-ninth birthdays later this year.

I stood up on the rung of a stool to get a better look. He was also playing bass guitar. He wore a black T-shirt and torn camouflage pants tucked into tall, black combat boots and held up by a silver-studded black belt. Tattoos galore extended from beyond his shirtsleeves. The whole combination gave him a hardcore look of a total badass. Dangerous and sexy.

My mouth half dropped as I listened, entranced, to his voice. And his face. It should be a crime to look so good and yet sing so hardcore.

As if reading my thoughts, the guitarist launched into a punk riff, transforming the song to a hard-and-heavy tempo and diverting my attention to him. While the singer had more of a military/punk rock look, the guitarist's outfit seemed more like a costume. He sported a brown, sleeveless tunic that covered his torso and ended in strips over his upper thighs after being fastened by a thick black belt with a giant silver piece. His legs were bare and his feet were covered with giant black boots covered with spikes. With his mussed-up shoulder-length hair, he looked as if he stepped out of another time and place, like from one of those fantasy video games. I pictured him wielding a giant, silver, jeweled sword or some other weapon rather than the modern electric guitar he shredded the new tune on.

The drummer had the Velvet Cocks logo on his drum set —a rooster wearing a smoking jacket and an ornate V and C, which appeared very Victorian and proper. Misdirection perhaps as to the actual naughty words?

The singer followed suit and his croon turned from soft and haunting to an almost primal scream of yearning. The singer motioned to a couple of people in the crowd.

"Come on up here for the next song. I think we all know this one. We put our spin on it. Come on, everyone now, sing along."

The Velvet Cocks then sang a version of *Witchcraft*, only their style was fast and heavy, so unlike Frank Sinatra's version it was like another song. The two women he pulled onstage were on either side of him now, singing along. I turned away from them to face the bar as I became aware I had started feeling uncomfortable.

Why? I focused once again on my drink as if I'd find some insight there. But then I was afraid of what I'd come up with so I focused on the crowd.

Some songs later, the two women who had climbed onstage approached a couple of men at the bar. I hadn't noticed the men before, but they were both attractive, although in different ways. One was dark and somewhat mysterious looking with eyes always on the move, scanning the entire club. The lighter one sported facial stubble and looked far more suave and comfortable in his surroundings. The tall woman with straight black hair and bangs spoke to the dark one while the one with auburn hair walked up to the other one. Their close stances clearly signaled they were couples. For some reason this made me feel better knowing neither of the women were with the singer. I didn't want to analyze why.

A woman near me spoke loudly enough to her friend for me to overhear. "I think that guy's the owner. And that's his girlfriend." When I followed who she was looking at, it was the dark-haired couple.

Her friend replied, "But didn't the other guy near him own this club before the fire?"

"Yeah, I think you're right. I haven't seen him here for a long time."

Fire? What fire? Obviously these women had been regulars for a while to know the club's history and who's who.

When the set ended, Ally found me at the bar. "Awesome, right?" she said.

"Yeah, they're cool," I said with a shrug.

"Did you see the guitar player? Chee Keydood. He's so friggin' hot it almost kills me. I want to run my fingers through his mussed-up hair and oooh." She scrunched her hand to mimic the action.

Ally waved a twenty-dollar bill at the bar. It didn't take long for her to get noticed by the male bartender although several others were vying for his and other bartenders' attention. With her long blonde hair and a dress so short and tight that it left nothing to the imagination, I doubt anyone that night could ignore Ally.

"Nice name." I took a sip of my drink. "I couldn't see too well. But yeah, he looked all right. Not my type though. I'm not into guys with long hair."

She widened her eyes as if I were crazy. "I guess that's why we're such good friends. We have such different taste in guys that we'd never fight over the same one."

"Guess so." I smiled and took a sip. "I thought the singer was pretty cute."

"Leggy Bones? Really? Guess that proves my point."

"Leggy Bones?" I repeated. "That's his name? Where do they come up with these names?"

"Stage name, obviously. They're a bunch of cheeky bastards." As the bartender walked over, Ally looked at my glass. "Ready for another drink?"

I shook my head. "I still have this one."

"We need to celebrate your promotion. Check you out—still in your twenties and already a director," she said. "Not bad for a bookworm."

"I'm barely still in my twenties. And I'm not just a bookworm. I go out."

"Oh real-ly," Ally said with skepticism dripping from the end of the drawn-out word.

"Yes. I go—places."

"Going to bookstores or the gym doesn't count as going out. I mean out-out. Nightlife. Music. Dancing. Like this."

"Well, I'm here now."

"Yes, we are. Now let's check out the eye candy after I get my drink." While Ally ordered her drink, I scanned the club. Most of the crowd stuck around after the band played and the DJ took over. He began with a short, fast song to keep the energetic vibe. Also to keep the people around who only came to see the show, I imagine.

After the bartender brought Ally her drink, she said, "A toast. To my beautiful, brilliant, best friend. Congratulations. You worked hard to get here and you deserve it."

I tried not to blush. "Thanks, Ally."

"What are we celebrating?" a male voice interrupted from behind me.

I rolled my eyes at Ally as if to say *can you believe it.* Some guy totally creeping in on my time celebrating with my girl-friend. However, she was widening her eyes in a *shut up, shut up* gesture.

Why? It wasn't that shocking to have some guy hitting on you in a club.

"*We* are *not* celebrating anything," I said sharply as I turned to face the intruder. Then my voice caught in my throat when I processed the interruption was spoken by a male with a slight English accent.

Yes, it was him. The singer of the Velvet Cocks. His face had appeared angelic under the spotlights up onstage. Now that he was only a foot from me, I saw a downright mischievous look about him, from the twinkle in his eye down to a slight smirk on his lips. His eyes were a bright hazel. I couldn't miss the color and intensity highlighted by the lights in the bar area. And those lashes—so dark and thick.

"Oh, I apologize if I was interrupting. I thought I heard your friend here lauding your accomplishments and just wanted to extend my congratulations."

Shit. I didn't have to sound so cold. I could be such a bitch sometimes. Ugh. I replaced my haughty expression with one a little more neutral.

Something bothered me when he spoke. I didn't expect it —the language he used. Lauding accomplishments? He spoke rather—what was it—educated? Not what I thought a punk rocker would sound like. I knew that was an unfair generalization, but in my defense, he belted out some crazy-ass lyrics onstage.

"You heard correctly," Ally said. "My friend hates having attention focused on her and gets all crabby about it."

Besides his sultry voice and rugged good looks, his scent was unbelievably alluring. My inner kitty purred at the mixture of the salty sweat from playing onstage and the distinctive musk of a human male. I resisted the urge to lean in and inhale.

Leggy laughed. "And then a strange bloke sticks his nose into the mix to bring even more attention."

"We're celebrating her promotion."

He turned to me. "That is a cause for celebration. Well done. Would you allow me to buy you champagne?"

"Um, no, that's not necess—" I began, but then Ally cut me off.

"How generous of you. Yes, we'd love that."

While he ordered champagne from the female bartender, I shot Ally a look. She continued the silent eye conversation by opening her eyes wide and nodding toward him. I opened my eyes wider in return, only my expression meant *What the heck are you saying?* She shook her head and turned to focus on Leggy. When the bartender returned with two glasses, he handed them to Ally and me.

"What about you?" I asked.

"This is for you lovely ladies," he said. "And I will excuse myself to allow you to celebrate. Congratulations." He bowed slightly. "I'm sure you deserve all the accolades—and then many more. Good night, ladies."

Accolades? What kind of rock singer speaks this way? Wasn't he just singing about fucking in the streets of Paris?

He moved into the crowd. I watched him until he disappeared among the black- clad dancers.

I realized too late we hadn't thanked him.

After we toasted and took a sip of the champagne, Ally said. "Well, spank me cross- eyed! That was nice. Leggy Bones buying us champagne."

"Yes, it was." I circled the edge of the glass. "We didn't even thank him."

"Shit, you're right. He disappeared so quickly. Weird that he didn't stay for a drink."

"Maybe he was just being a gentleman," I said.

Ally rolled her eyes. "A lead singer of a rock band? Get real. He doesn't have to be a gentleman. I'm sure he can get laid whenever he wants."

Good point. "Well, I don't know. How do you explain his generous gesture then?"

Ally thought. "Beats me. But I wish it was Chee Keydood. And that I was drinking champagne with him and not you right now."

"Ally!"

"Just kidding."

"Come on, let's dance. Finally."

"Oh stop it," Ally said with a wave. "I've been dancing all night."

We squeezed in through the uninhibited bodies dancing wildly to a Prodigy song, *Smack My Bitch Up*. After that strong drink, my inhibitions were lowered. I finally shook my booty the way I'd been itching to do all night. But thoughts of that singer invaded my mind. I caught myself looking for him several times, to no avail.

"Who are you looking for?" Ally asked, letting me know how conspicuous my peeking really was.

"Oh nobody. Just checking out the goods."

She glanced around. "Plenty of good things to see tonight."

She was right. Forget that guy. He's the singer of a rock band. Probably being entertained backstage by a trio of women in revealing outfits at that very moment. I diverted my attention to some of the other guys in the club. Plenty of eye candy on the dance floor and they moved their bodies well, which meant they might be skillful with their bodies in other ways. It had been too long since I had a lover and my kind had a higher sex drive than most humans. Unbearably high at times. What I needed now was a lover to help me cope. Not a boyfriend, not any sort of relationship other than one to fulfill our sexual desires.

Win-win for everyone.

*****

"Love your dress," a male voice said. One I recognized as the one who had commanded the crowd earlier and who had bought us champagne. My body temperature rose.

I turned to face him on the dance floor and said, "Thanks."

This tight little black-and-red plaid number was one of my favorites, but I didn't dare wear it often. Then, at a loss for words, I commanded myself, *speak*. "I see you're a fan of plaid yourself." I nodded at his hat. "I found this dress in a vintage store in Harvard Square."

I said speak, not babble. Why would a guy care where you bought a dress?

I'd stopped dancing once he arrived, but with him now swaying in front of me, I felt like an idiot. Something about him was so disarming that I couldn't just size him up, put him into a neat little category into my brain. I joined him and resumed dancing, forcing myself to breathe properly and move naturally. Whatever song was playing was slow enough and not as loud as the other ones so we could hear each other.

"Yes, you can still get some excellent finds there even though a lot of rubbish chain stores have moved in."

What were we talking about again? My brain raced to catch up.

"I love the bookstores there, too," he continued. "You can find some rare out-of- print books." I raised my eyebrows to indicate my surprise at a rock singer perusing bookstores, but he didn't notice. "There aren't as many places to shop as there once were. But this baby is a classic." He motioned to indicate my dress. Then he looked me up and down. If I didn't know he was checking out my dress, I might have had a few words for the unabashed eye-fuck. "Schoolgirl chick meets rock 'n' roll. Nice yet naughty all at once."

Surprised he'd be that interested in my outfit, I teased, "You're really into women's dresses."

He laughed. "I'm going to bow out on replying *I'd like to be in your dress right now*, although you clearly set yourself up for that one."

My mouth dropped open in an indignant protest.

"Not women's dresses per se," he continued, "but I need to keep my eyes open for eye-catching outfits to wear onstage."

"You're the singer, right?" What a dumb question. One I already knew the answer to. And one he probably thought was stupid, as I clearly should have noticed the singer of the band playing in the club that night.

He didn't call me out on it, luckily, but answered. "I am. Leggy Bones. My stage name. Don't worry, my parents didn't hate me that much to name me Leggy."

"Do I dare ask your real name?"

"I'll only tell you mine if you tell me yours."

217

"Somehow I have the feeling you've used this line on women before."

"Not a bad way to introduce one's self, don't you think? It's better than the *I'm so- and-so. Nice to meet you* bull."

I shrugged. "It gets to the point quickly though, doesn't it? And who has time to waste these days?"

"I suppose."

"I didn't get a chance to thank you for the champagne. That was very sweet of you. Thank you." I put my hand on his shoulder to show my appreciation, but my gesture backfired as jolts of excitement ricocheted back to me, throwing me off.

"No problem." He nodded. "Hope you and your friend enjoyed it."

"We did."

"So what is it then?"

"What's what?"

"Your name."

"Oh." I thought for a moment. "You know what? I could probably make up any name right now that I wanted. It's not as if it matters, right?"

"Are you always this obstinate?" he asked.

I scrunched up my face a little. "I would say no. But my family often calls me stubborn or pigheaded. I like obstinate better."

"Don't make that face. You look too cute like that. You're distracting me from the question."

"Question? What question?" I tilted my head and smiled up at him.

"You're being coy."

"Why don't we say it's Cara?"

"We can say Cara, but we both know that's not your name. However, if you want to play that way, nice to meet you, Cara. I'm Leggy."

We stared at each other for several long moments, our eyes searching each other's as we sized the other up.

"I don't understand why you really want to know," I said. "You'll forget it five minutes after I tell you. I mean, you're a singer of a rock band. But I'm not a groupie. So if you're looking to pick someone up for the night, you're better off looking elsewhere."

I was on the hunt for a longer-term sex partner, not a one-night stand.

He laughed, throwing his head back. "A groupie? Come on now."

"I'm serious. I'm not going to go home with you no matter how generous you were with the champagne gesture."

"Settle down, tiger. I'm not hitting on you."

My internal radar went up. Why did he use a feline reference? Did he sense something about me?

"I'm just a computer geek who mustered up the nerve to talk to a pretty lady," he said.

Ah, perhaps not. It was just a saying.

"Ha ha. Funny." I looked at his outfit, which clearly screamed bad rock 'n' roller, a far cry from someone calling himself a computer geek. "Okay, Mr. IT, I'm sure I'm completely wrong. And you have a bunch of computers and servers backstage rather than a bunch of groupies."

He took a deep inhale and exhaled slowly before responding. "Just because I'm a singer of a rock band doesn't mean I have a gaggle of groupies backstage."

Gaggle of groupies? I raised my eyebrows again to indicate my skepticism. This time he caught it.

"Listen, I'm not some rock 'n' roll cliché." The half-smile that had been on his face until now disappeared into a grim line. "I am a real person, not a caricature of one. Perhaps I overheard a couple of beautiful women at the bar celebrating what sounded to be a momentous moment. I was feeling pretty good after a great set and wanted to do something nice for someone else."

A part of me felt like shit as he did seem sincere. But another part of me was wary. That could be his well-rehearsed excuse, just part of his shtick to seduce unsuspecting women.

"Well, if that's true. I thank you once again. Like I said, it was sweet."

He took that half-bow once again. "Good night, Cara. It was nice not quite meeting the real you."

"Good night, Leggy. It was also nice not quite meeting the real you."

He looked at me for another moment and then left. I wanted to stomp my own foot with my stupid weapon-like heels.

Did I just blow it?

Nico

Damn, that woman was hot.

Yet so cold and dismissive. Which made her all the more intriguing.

I shook my head as I walked away. *Why am I always chasing the ones who are clearly not interested?*

"Leggy, great show tonight. You were awesome!" An attractive blonde in a tight black dress walked alongside me.

"Cara" was right; I bet I could ask this woman to come home with me tonight and she wouldn't even think twice about it.

"Thanks," I said. "I appreciate you coming out to see us."

"Can we have a drink?" she asked. Her eyes were filled with expectation.

The battle that raged inside me every time I was approached by a pretty woman started up anew.

She's hot. You should go for it. It's not as if you've never done it before.

Yeah, but that got old pretty quickly. What's the point of sleeping with someone who is only into you because you're in a band? Most guys would be all over that. They loved having a girl or two in every city. Juggling women was a pastime. All that drama sounded exhausting. The awkward moments post-sex always made me cringe.

Perhaps I'm not most guys. Perhaps I've had enough meaningless encounters. It's time for something more in a woman.

"Another time, perhaps. I'm going to head backstage to cool down after that set."

"I could come with you. Keep you company?"

"You're a beautiful girl. But I'm kind of beat and need to be alone for a little while."

She didn't bother to hide her disappointment. Then she put on a brave smile and walked away.

I watched her walk away—tall, lean body in that tight dress.

What's wrong with me? I must be turning into a big old fogy in my thirties.

My thoughts diverted to the curvy brunette. Then to my hands running over the curves underneath that dress.

A woman who shot you down earlier. A woman who wouldn't even tell you her real name.

Maybe I'd capture her interest if I bent her over my lap and gave her a good spanking.

Ha, as if that would ever happen. She is clearly not interested in you. Yet you're still thinking about her? What a sucker for punishment you are.

Lily

When I caught myself thinking about my conversation with Leggy at work that week, I tried not to cringe and quickly forced myself to think of something else. Luckily, work was good for distraction from daily life. My laptop kept me busy with emails to answer, documents to write up, and software to learn.

After work, however, it was a different story. I'd log in my usual hour at the gym, shower and come home for dinner. Many nights I picked up something at the healthy fast food café next to the gym, but sometimes I became adventurous and tried to experiment with whatever vegetables I picked up from the farmers' market, convincing myself I could actually cook. Some of these experiments worked out well and others— well, I ended up picking up something at the café after all. Since it was January in New England, the farmers' markets were long over so my kitchen went into hibernation.

Once I was back home in my apartment, I thought about him. What's he like? What's his life like? What's he doing now? Is he with some girl who had fallen all over him the night before? I mean, it wouldn't be hard—look at me thinking about him and I wasn't even a fan of the band.

Before I could stop myself, I was checking their website. Surely this wouldn't be considered cyberstalking, right? I mean, it is a public website out there for the world to visit.

Leggy appeared on the homepage. I stared for who knew how long. The other band members were pictured there as well, but my gaze was fixed on Leggy in a pair of torn-up gray camouflage cargo shorts, red suspenders dangling down over them, a black tank top and black combat boots. I scanned the contours of his face, etching them into memory. And his eyes. The mischievous look that I remembered from that night at Vamps was hinted at in his eyes as he stared right back at me.

My eyes scanned down his body. The lean muscles in his tattooed arms. The tank top was tight enough to reveal he didn't carry an ounce of fat on him. I pictured what his abs must look like underneath. With the definition elsewhere, I'd bet money he had a six-pack that begged to be explored by my fingers.

And his shorts. I caught myself staring at the bulge between his legs and blushed even though nobody was there to know.

I clicked on the bio page. It didn't contain any personal info about individual members, but gave a brief history of the band.

Velvet Cocks formed five years ago as a dare between a bunch of computer geeks. Some guys at a software company north of Boston were looking for a way to unwind after staring at a computer screen all day. Three of them—two software engineers and an IT tech—decided to form a rock band. Everything about them was tongue-in-cheek at first—who could come up with a raunchy band name, clever stage name, wildest outfit—as a sort of slam and homage to the rock and punk bands they grew up listening to. The dare turned into something bigger as they realized they actually played pretty well. Nobody was more surprised about this than they were. In addition to playing their own twists on classic songs, they started writing original songs, especially in reference to the computer world they worked in and the books they read. Soon they began touring underground clubs in New England at any place that would book them. To their shock, regulars started coming to see them. After a few years, they were signed to record their first album. They recently released their second album, which they are promoting with shows in New England, New York, and DC. Still geeks at heart, they kept their day jobs working on computer technology.

Shit, he was telling the truth about being a computer geek. Interesting. I leaned back and ran my index finger over my lower lip. I never would have guessed any of that about them.

Perhaps I'd been wrong to peg him as a groupie magnet and all. I should not have made some sweeping generalizations based on someone's appearance. Ugh, I was a cynical shit too quick to rush to judgment. Especially when it came to guys.

I clicked on the link for their music page and clicked Play to start a playlist of some of their songs. As I tidied up my apartment, Leggy's voice either screamed out lyrics in hard, fast songs or crooned softly through the slower ones. Hearing the song in my apartment rather than a loud club, I could make out more of the lyrics. I chuckled at a modern-day banter between Holmes and Watson.

The song *Never Trust a Woman with an Asp* was a punk rock homage to the tragic love between Antony and Cleopatra. There was a witty exchange between Anne Rice's brooding vampire Louis and the rock 'n' roll Lestat in *Vampire Bromance.* Then there was that crowd pleaser *Let's Fuck All Over Paris*—the one song I recognized from seeing them play live. Listening to the lyrics now, I started to figure out the references. The vagabonds and prostitutes. The joy of having nothing and the bleak despair of being alone. Tropic of Cancer. Duh, now I got it. It was an ode to Henry Miller's sexual romps in France.

Ally was right; they were a bunch of cheeky bastards.

Other songs included short punk rants against politics and corporate tactics that hurt workers. Even though I thought the lyrics were rather clever, most of all I was taken by his voice. Damn, his voice was sexy. Whether he was waxing poetic odes to literary masterpieces or criticizing corporate greed, his voice oozed a sensuality that crept right under my skin.

I was tempted to Google Leggy himself to find more about him, but then I admonished myself to stop cyber-stalking and slammed my laptop shut.

Stop acting like a teenage girl with a crush on some rock star. You're a professional. You're not sixteen. You have a career. Maybe it's been too long since you've had a lover. Maybe you need to get online at one of those dating sites. It's better than meeting some guy in some club, especially some unattainable rock star.

After work, I went to the gym to hit one of Ally's classes. She texted me earlier while I was at work and asked if I wanted to go out for a walk after class. We often met for a walk or a drink. Sometimes we'd offset the calories we'd burned off in class with whatever junk food Ally wanted to consume, or feed my addiction to cookies. With her ridiculous metabolism, Ally ate whatever she wanted, which was usually something picked up at Dunkin' Donuts. She was the kind of woman that most women wanted to hate because of that fact. However, with her bubbly and outgoing personality it was impossible to do so. She had great genes.

I, on the other hand, had to stick to the healthy food or else I'd blow up to a pear shape overnight. My weakness was cookies though and I was not going to cut my craving for cookies no matter what the consequence. I'd cut out all the other good fatty foods; let me have my one indulgence.

Oreos, chocolate chip, oatmeal raisin, Fig Newtons... I could go on. My favorite time of year was Christmas and not for all the gift-giving; it was the cookie swaps.

Ally and I had met at the gym. She taught yoga and Pilates classes there and I went to her classes a couple of times a week. We'd become pals one night after class when we both stopped by the juice bar. Even though we were polar opposites personality-wise, appearance-wise ,and just about any way you could think of, we hit it off and became friends. She was a fit strawberry-blonde, tattooed, outgoing animal lover. Everything about me was darker, from looks to personality. I was far more introverted and private, not close to many people besides my mom, but she lived in New Hampshire.

With my secret, the more distance I kept between people, the better.

Unlike Ally, I did not have any pets. Who would take care of it when I had to leave town? That was my practical excuse. The real reason was that animals sensed I was different. Dogs often barked like mad when I walked by them in the park and their owners would apologize, being perplexed. "I don't know what's gotten into her. She rarely barks."

And cats. They wouldn't come near me.

Tonight, Ally and I headed down to walk on the trails at the nearby lake. She was dressed in yoga pants and a fitted pink tank top with a matching pink workout jacket, which accentuated her slim figure. Her hair was piled up on the top of her head into a messy bun and held by a clip. If I tried to pin my hair up that way, it would look like I suffered through an apocalypse. She probably did it without even looking in the mirror and of course it looked casual yet chic on her.

Must be nice being her. Eat whatever you want, look great, and work in a low-stress environment. No furry little problem that pops up once a month, making you hide from society.

"Did you have fun the other night?" she asked.

"Yes, I did. Thanks for bringing me there. That club was wild."

"It didn't freak you out too much?"

"No, not at all. Maybe you're right. Maybe I am a closet freak."

"Oh, you definitely are," she said and then took a swig from her water bottle. "Everyone knows it's always the quiet ones."

Trying to sound nonchalant, I said, "It was cool of that singer to buy us champagne."

"Yeah, it was," she said. "Didn't I see him talking to you on the dance floor later?"

"Uhhhh," I didn't want to replay the conversation. The one where I came off as a bitch—again—for not telling him my name. "He liked my dress. We talked about where to find clothes."

She raised her eyebrows. "The singer of a punk rock band was asking you for fashion tips? Obviously he doesn't know how conservatively you dress at work."

"I'm a professional. I can't dress in some slutty outfit in the office."

"How about in the gym? You and your shorts and T-shirts. You have a killer body you're hiding. Why not show it off?"

"I'm there to work out, not show anything. But thanks, must be all the running that's helped," I teased.

"Must be all the yoga and Pilates from an awesome instructor." "Oh yeah." I chuckled. "That's it." "So did anything else happen? With Leggy Bones?" "Um, no."

"Aww, I was hoping you'd say you gave him your number or something. And how you've been secretly banging like monkeys ever since."

Ooh. Was my fantasy that transparent? My cheeks burned.

"Come on. You know that's not true. I left with you that night. No secret lover for me, I'm afraid."

"You should get one. You work too much. And a secret lover is as exciting as hell."

One person came to mind. He had a slight British accent and an impressive vocabulary.

Too bad I'd brushed him off and hadn't even given him my name.

Chapter Two

The snows of January melted in the first week of February only to return with greater gusto the following week. Like the rest of the non-skiers in New England, I coped with the snow, dreaming about spring. The weeks went by, the snow melted, and I thought of the enigmatic Leggy Bones less and less. Although he still crept into my mind at the oddest of moments, especially when I was alone in the evenings in my condo, the rational side of me forced thoughts of him out. *He's a rock star; you're just one of many fantasizing about him. You're wasting your time.*

I moved on with my daily life as usual, burying myself with work and Ally's gym classes during the week and then finding a way to unwind on the weekends. Most of the time, this meant more time at the gym and then a bookstore to find a book to lose myself in. It wasn't a wild life, but one I was content with. And a way to have an attempt at normalcy to compensate for what I had to deal with during the full moon, I typically hid in the mountains up north where it was safer than staying near the city.

Occasionally I drove into Cambridge or Boston to browse around in funky little shops and bookstores, but today I stayed nearby in Salem, Massachusetts, good ol' Witch City USA, where I would find some fun, eclectic reads at the Wiccan or touristy bookshops. I loved the ghost stories they printed up of old haunted New England, even though if I read them too late, they'd keep me up at night. Salem wasn't too crowded at this time of the year. As the winter was winding down, the streets were relatively quiet and I found a parking spot on the main road easily. New England winters were not known for their hospitality to residents or tourists. I imagine the only sane visitors to New England during the winter were skiers and snowboarders and since Salem didn't have any ski mountains, the tourists were gone for the season.

Today, the winds were calm enough off the Atlantic Ocean that I was warm enough in my LL Bean coat and gloves, but still breezy enough that only a few other pedestrians walked along the shore. I took pleasure in the lack of crowds. Once spring was in full swing, the sidewalks of Salem would be chock-a-block with tourists clamoring to learn more about the Witch City and the history of the Salem witch trials. The traditional witch museums and historical tours remained year after year, but new attractions sprang up all the time. Eclectic stores specialized in witchcraft items, wizard lore and pirate themes. Ghost tours and other attractions designed to scare visitors popped up.

After having a coffee and muffin at a café near the Salem Willows, I wandered down to a bookstore in the main part of town. I scanned the new releases in search of something to sink into while I did my laundry this afternoon. What an exciting weekend I had planned, I thought wryly.

"What an oddly pleasant surprise," a man said. "Fancy seeing you again, Cara."

Cara? Why did that name ring a bell?

Oh shit—that was the fake name I used. Just once. With one person. Who had that faint British accent.

I glanced up quickly to verify it was him. Those hazel eyes staring at me confirmed my hope or fear or whatever emotion it was that vied for dominance. He disarmed me. I was mesmerized by the earthy-brown on the outer edge of his irises that faded into a mossy-green gradient closer to the pupil. Then I looked down since the next emotion that flooded in was guilt. Even though his band's website was public, I couldn't help but think I'd been snooping.

"I'm surprised you remembered," I said, finally finding the sense to respond.

Looking away from his face wasn't enough to distract me from his presence because then I assessed his body. He was wearing normal clothes—faded jeans and a black T-shirt with a white skull on it. The shirt was just tight enough for me to make out a cut torso beneath. A tattoo of the VC scrolled logo extended from under his sleeve.

Hmm, what other tattoos did he have hidden under his clothes?

"How could I not? You made it so difficult to get even a fake name out of you."

He smiled and it made me blush for reasons I didn't quite understand. What I did know was that he still looked hot as hell. Even hotter now than he did onstage. A literary bad boy in a bookstore.

And smelled even more intoxicating. Although the scent of his masculinity and the sweat from playing onstage had elicited an involuntary sensual response from me the first time we met, now I found it even more difficult not to bury my face in his neck. I would inhale the heady fragrance of him, the faint scent of soap lingering on him. I'd bet it was Irish Spring.

Act normal. Act normal.

"What can I say?" I recovered quickly. "I guess I'm a private person. And I don't give out my personal information to someone I just met. Not even to computer geeks who double as rock stars."

I flashed him a smile, which was a mistake. He looked at me so intensely that I forgot my intention of flirting as my mind now swarmed with questions. Time sped up and slowed all at once. Why was he looking at me that way? Did he realize the effect he was having upon me? What the heck was happening? Whatever it was, I didn't like this feeling of being out of control.

I had to break the eye contact to gain some perspective on the situation. But when I looked down, I made the unfortunate mistake of looking directly at his crotch, which threw me off-kilter in a different way.

"Find anything promising?" he asked.

My cheeks burned. *Oh God, yes! There is so much promise right there.*

"Umm." I looked up at him again.

"A book," he clarified. "Did you find any promising reads?"

~

I hope you enjoyed this excerpt of Ignite. *It will be released soon!*
PREORDER NOW!

ACKNOWLEDGMENTS

As always, I am so grateful to everyone who helps make each book possible, helping me shape the ideas in my head into a story. Huge thanks to my fellow authors, critique partners, editors, beta readers, ARC readers, Street Team, and you, the reader!

ABOUT THE AUTHOR

USA Today Bestselling author Lisa Carlisle loves stories with dark, brooding heroes and spirited heroines. She is thrilled to be a multi-published author since she's wanted to write since the sixth grade. Her travels and many jobs have provided her with inspiration for novels, such as deploying to Okinawa, Japan, backpacking alone around Europe, or working as a waitress in Paris. Her love of books inspired her to own a small independent book store for a couple of years. Lisa now lives in New England with her husband, children, two kittens, and many fish.

Sign up for her VIP list to hear about new releases, specials, and freebies:
www.lisacarlislebooks.com/subscribe/

Visit her website for more on books, trailers, playlists, and more:
Lisacarlislebooks.com

Lisa loves to connect with readers. You can find her on:
Facebook
Twitter - @lisacbooks
Pinterest
Instagram
Goodreads

Knights of Stone: Mason
Highland Gargoyles 1

A Romance Reads Top Pick!

Few have ever dared to cross the boundaries--until now...

With a quarter century of burning hatred between the inhabitants of the Isle of Stone, Kayla knows all too well it is forbidden to cross boundaries. But that doesn't keep her from being sorely tempted.

Drawn to discover the secrets beyond the tree witches' forest, Kayla is intrigued by the talk of unconventional rock concerts in gargoyle territory.

But when she risks everything to sneak away from the coven, she never expects to return night after night, not just for the music, but for one particular gargoyle who captured her heart with his guitar.

Nor did she expect that her attention had not gone unnoticed...

With plans to seduce the pixie-like female, Mason spent several nights keeping a watchful eye on his prize, unaware she's not just a passing visitor. But when he discovers she's a tree witch, an enemy to his entire kind, Mason knows that anything between them would be forbidden. No matter how strong the temptation...

But other elements command their attention.

Something much more dangerous haunts the wolf shifters of the isle....

With the magic veil thinning there will be blood... and the full moon is coming.

Knights of Stone: Mason is the first book in a shifter paranormal romance series with a Highland touch and a hard hit of rock romance. If you like hot men in kilts, dark paranormal thrills, and forbidden love, then you'll be hooked by the Highland Gargoyles Series!

Other books in the Highland Gargoyles series:

- **Knights of Stone: Mason**
- **Knights of Stone: Lachlan**
- **Knights of Stone: Bryce**
- **Seth - a wolf shifter romance in the series**
- **Knights of Stone: Calum**

Chateau Seductions, a Paranormal Erotic Romance Series

Darkness Rising

Antoine Chevalier harbors a secret. Born a gargoyle shifter, he wants nothing more than to cultivate his art. His hard work pays off the night he completes his greatest sculpture. But the excitement of his accomplishment doesn't last.

He's drawn the eye of the wrong group—a clan of vampires. Antoine wakes into darkness, changed. Shattered. His dream of becoming a renowned sculptor is destroyed.

One question remains—how will he ever survive an eternity of darkness alone?

Darkness Rising is part 0.5 of the Chateau Seductions series by USA Today Bestselling author Lisa Carlisle. Readers have requested more on the dark and mysterious Antoine. In this short story, Antoine tells his tale, which continues in the series with Dark Velvet. Dark Velvet is written from Savannah's perspective as a newcomer to an art colony who is intrigued by the proprietor.

Read Now!

Dark Velvet

Grad student Savannah Evans is thrilled to be accepted as a resident to a prestigious art colony. Where else would she be able to focus on her craft of writing poetry in a setting like that of the medieval-styled castle? The remote New England island is a respite from her hectic city life. When she meets her benefactor, a mysterious French sculptor, her expectations for carefree days writing near the ocean are distracted by unprofessional fantasies about her sponsor.

Antoine Chevalier built Les Beaux Arts on DeRoche Island to bring purpose back to an existence that has lost meaning. He's wandered the earth for decades and finds solace in returning to art. When Savannah applies for a residency, something about her words touches him. After her arrival, a physical attraction grows between them, which he struggles against. She deserves more than someone of his kind.

Antoine proposes they become lovers during her stay. But the situation turns complicated when Savannah discovers his secret. She had suspicions about his identity, but finds the truth overwhelming. Consumed by her desire for Antoine and faced with a tough decision, she is blind to the danger that has arrived at DeRoche Island.

"Dark Velvet has a dark eroticism that makes you want to be Savannah. It is a book that is a good, quick and darkly thrilling read." ~ Books and Beyond Fifty Shades

"...insanely hot chemistry between the female protagonist Savannah & vampire Antoine. Their intensity starts off right away and you're not a chapter in before it takes off like a rocket!" ~ Paranormal Romance Junkies

Read Now!

Dark Muse

It takes time before Gina Meiro warms up to people and her shyness is often misunderstood. She hasn't had to worry about meeting new people at a remote art colony until a new resident arrives—a rock guitarist more suited for a billboard. Her carefree days of painting at the medieval-styled castle on a remote New England island are shattered when she stumbles right into his welcome gathering.

After a falling out with his band, Dante Riani wants nothing more at Les Beaux Arts on DeRoche Island than solitude to work on new songs. When a shy young painter asks to paint him at sunset, he's tempted by the opportunity to be alone with her.

Someone at the colony claims to know what Dante is and asks for his help. Dante fears his plans are coming undone, especially as grows more drawn to Gina. Her scent and vulnerability are too difficult to resist. But he must stay away from her—she would never understand his secret.

While it is a story about struggle, it is also about love; and doing whatever needs to be done to be with the one you are attracted to. I really enjoyed the dynamic between Gina and Dante. This story has the perfect amount of witty banter, sex, and romance."

~ 5* Review of Dark Muse from Books and Beyond Fifty Shades!

Read Now!

Dark Stranger

Wolf shifters come to Chateau seeking a missing pack member. During an altercation, Cameron Stevens, the manager of the art colony, is separated from the others. He ends up alone with Nadya, one of the female shifters.

Together, in the forests of DeRoche Island, they struggle against conflicting feelings. In addition to battling each other as well as their mistrust, they fight a powerful, inexplicable attraction to one another—one that leaves them irrevocably entwined.

They're mates? Cameron can't comprehend or accept such a thing is possible. They're two different species and their worlds don't mesh. He can't fight the heated desire burning between them and her touch is impossible to resist. His heart and mind aren't on the same page where she's concerned. One thing is certain—Nadya is stamped on both.

**** FIVE STARS ***** – "I have read the first 2 books in this series and could not wait to get my hands on this one; and I was not disappointed. The thing I love most, is that while this is a story about paranormal creatures, you can still relate to the trial and tribulations that they go through. You can relate to how each character is feeling, even though you are nothing like them."

~ **Books and Beyond Fifty Shades**

Read Now!

Temptation Returns

Antonio returns from the Marine Corps to begin a new life as a civilian. While visiting Cape Cod, he meets a strange woman who reads his Tarot cards. He doesn't believe in such nonsense; after all, he's a Marine. When he returns to Boston, he receives a ticket to a rock club where he runs into the one woman he never forgot.

Lina can't believe Antonio is back in town, right before her wedding. Being around him again resurrects long-buried feelings. Will she be able to resist temptation in the form of a dark-haired Italian Marine, the same man who once broke her heart?

4.5 Hearts from Books and Bindings

"This saucy little story hit the spot with interesting characters, some humor, some spice, and a thoughtful NA second chance love story about a returning vet with a few issues."

"I enjoyed the story, humor, and steam – oh yeah, did I mention the spice? Let's mention it again just to be safe."

Read Now!

Dress Blues

Sometimes it all comes down to timing...

Volunteering at a cat shelter is much calmer than the adrenaline-fueled skirmishes of Vivi Parker's last deployment in the Marines, but her limp is a constant reminder of what she endured. The shelter is her sanctuary, her one relief from memories that haunt her. At a fundraiser, she runs into a man she could never have while she served, but had never forgotten.

Active duty had its challenges, but starting over as a civilian in Boston is more difficult than Jack Conroy anticipated. When his mom and sister drag him to a cat benefit, he never expects to see a woman he last saw in Dress Blues--a woman he couldn't have, but could never forget.

Vivi fears she's no longer the woman Jack was drawn to, able to tackle rock climbing walls or other outdoor challenges. And Jack has decisions he must face.

Military rules forbade their burgeoning passion. But now, years later, the rules have changed.

Yet, so have they.

Is it ever too late for a second chance at love?

"Wow! Dress Blues is an awesome, fun, short must read in contemporary romantic fiction with a side of hot military characters and some sweet, fuzzy furballs!"

"An amazing story of two damaged Marines finding each other again."

"This is a fun, furry, feel good story of second chances... Ms. Carlisle's writing style grabs you from the first word and keeps you engaged with witty banter and sexy scenes. I loved this short second chance romance with a HEA and I'm sure you will too!"

Read Now!

Pursued

A Vampire Blood Courtesans Romance

A Night Owl Reviews Top Pick!

It was only meant to be three nights...

After watching my mother die, becoming a Blood Courtesan is key to my future in medicine. With loans racking up, all I have to do is pretend I want the money for tuition, and I'm hired. **No one can know the real reason for wanting this job.**

But it isn't as easy as it first seems. On my first night as a courtesan at a ball in Salem, I meet vampires for the first time--and flee.

Vampires are not easily dissuaded. And one in particular, Renato, offers me a proposal I find difficult to resist. He has a dark, smoldering appeal that lures me in. Plus, I might gain the insight I seek.

I'm supposed to provide a service and will be paid well for it. **But my feelings complicate our arrangement--and endanger my life.**

It was only meant to be three nights, but can I walk away now?

Welcome to the shadow world of Blood Courtesans...where vampires are real and blood is a commodity.

It's not supposed to be about love...until it is.

PURSUED is part of the Blood Courtesan series, starting with REBORN, Myra's story. See the full list of books here: bloodcourtesans.com.

Read Now!

When Darkness Whispers

A Romance Reads Top Pick!

Some memories are better left forgotten...

Haunted by an unclear past, biologically enhanced Marine, Eva

Montreaux, can't be distracted from her mission. With American servicemen being brutally murdered on the island of Okinawa, it's more than priority. It's critical. But when her investigation brings her face to face with Marcos Delacruz, it triggers memories. Ones she lost. Memories that somehow include him.

Marcos Delacruz has tried to forget the woman who left him with nothing but empty promises. Even now, three years later, Eva doesn't seem to express any guilt over breaking his heart. In truth, she seems to barely recognize him. This deployment has been challenging enough with too many restless spirits haunting the island. But when his own investigation forces him to cross paths with her once more, Marcos discovers there may be a deeper truth.

With the number of murders climbing rapidly and the rising need to track the murderer across the tropical island, Eva struggles to reclaim what she lost. But the island holds darker elements--a serial killer. One that doesn't appear to be human.

Thrust into a world she can't escape, Eva must discover a way to stop a murderer from destroying anyone else's future, but how can she succeed if she can't even remember what role Marcos played in her past?

When Darkness Whispers is full of paranormal romantic suspense you won't want to put down! Go undercover with a supernatural team into a world of vampires, gargoyles, shifters, demons, and ghosts. If you like haunting mystery, spine-tingling suspense, and Japanese mythology, you'll love When Darkness Whispers!

"Wow If I could give this story more than 5 stars I would... Suspense, Mystery, and Thrills all in one book." ~ Book Nook Nuts

Read Now!

Visit lisacarlislebooks.com for the latest releases, news, book trailers, and more!

Made in the USA
Middletown, DE
20 May 2018